Fang Fiction

Vampire Horror Stories

LM Kaplin

Broken Brain Books

BROKEN
BRAIN
BOOKS

Contents

For my Mom, the English teacher
and my Dad, who gave me my
first King book in middle school

FANG FICTION
VAMPIRE HORROR STORIES

L M Kaplin

The Garden Tomb

J erusalem
969 BC

Mara awoke from a violent shake. Her nostrils singed with the acrid smell of smoke that wafted through the open window next to her bed.

"Wake up! Quickly, we must go," her father said, releasing his hands from her shoulders.

"Where's mamma? What's happening?" Mara asked.

"She's gathering some things. Grab what you can. We have to leave now before the army reaches the city," Athan replied to his daughter.

The smoke that billowed in just after dawn gave early warning of King David's army marching toward their doorstep and the fires of destruction left in their wake. Athan, along with his wife and daughter, loaded anything they could into their cart and headed off in the opposite direction of the approaching army. It seemed almost everyone in the city had the same idea, as they quickly became caught in the congestion of people on the way out of town. Many families had carts such as Athan's, while others rode horses or donkeys. Some desperate families even walked, carrying whatever they could on their backs. The convergence of roads and mix of transportation methods brought everyone to a standstill as the great army neared the city. Panic set in as the soldiers drew closer. People began abandoning their carts and pushing past each other to escape. Some, trampled by the fleeing crowds, cried out as they fell to the ground.

Athan remained focused on his young daughter and held her close during the surge of people, but in the commotion became separated from his wife. He attempted to call out for her, but the din of the crowd made any attempt futile. Pushing against the mob of people to go back and look for her was also an impossibility. With no turning back, he pressed on, away from the army. The road, filled with people, abandoned carts and dropped belongings, became impassable and soon Athan found himself running in the sand, carrying his daughter as he went.

He ran until his legs neared the point of collapse, not knowing how long he'd been running for. Unable to go on like this, he put Mara down and slowed his pace to one that her little legs could manage. Until that point, escaping the army and keeping his daughter out of harm's way had been his only thought. Now, looking around, they were alone and safe for the time being. Continuing on, he pondered which direction to go. Their original plan had been to travel east to Jericho where they had family to stay with, but on foot, they would never make it that far. Turning around to get his bearings, Athan didn't recognize his surroundings. Panic set in while he continued to look for other people or a landmark along the horizon. Surprised that he didn't see other fleeing civilians, the heat overcame him, and Athan sat for a moment to dispel a bout of dizziness. He saw nothing except for a few unfamiliar rock formations and smoke from the fires behind him. His own footprints still marked the path leading to where he stood, but he could not go back the way they came.

Veering off to the left, he headed to the largest boulder in the distance. He knew of a few settlements nearby, and if this structure wasn't part of one, he could climb on top for a better view. That would surely point them in the right direction.

The trek took considerably longer than Athan had predicted. Mara kept them at a slow pace and as they walked, it seemed as if the rock stayed the same size, far off in the distance. Eventually, after many hours of walking in the desert sun, they approached and finally arrived at the rock. In the back of Athan's mind, he had hoped that the rock would be something more. Visions of a nice old lady in a hut with cold water flashed through his mind, but as they drew near, he knew his initial assessment had been correct.

Reaching the top of the rock would prove harder than Athan had expected. He could climb the side easily, but the sun's heat on the rock's surface burned his fingers, causing him to recoil in surprise upon grabbing hold. He took off his tattered shirt to use as protection and wrapped it around his hands while he climbed. With this, Athan made it to the top, although his exposed arms and chest suffered burns along the way.

The rock sat high enough, standing on top, gave Athan a greater line of vision, but his heart sank as he looked in each direction. From the top of the rock, he only had a better view of the vast nothingness that surrounded them. Losing hope, he wondered if they would have been better off staying home and begging the soldiers for mercy. At least then, he would share the same fate as his wife, instead of being left to wonder about her. There was no point in thinking about what ifs. It would soon be nightfall and they had no shelter for the evening.

With nothing else in sight, Athan decided the best course of action would be to make camp next to the rock. The hours of walking through the sand spent most of his energy. Mara had yet to complain, but he could see the fear on her face. He tried to comfort her, but didn't want to make any promises he couldn't keep. After a good night's sleep, they would set off at first light and find something. Sleep came easily to Athan. He'd had an excruciating day and knew tomorrow would be no different. His skin was tender from the sun, but the evening air felt cool. Too tired to dream, he slept with Mara curled up in his embrace.

Only a few hours into sleep and Athan awoke to a poking in his ribs. Coming out of a daze, it took him a moment to register that Mara had awoken him with a look of fear in her eyes. His ears perked up and instantly realized the reason for her nervousness. Athan knew the whooping sound well from living along the edge of the desert, but had never heard it this loud before. The sound echoed off the rock and could be heard from every direction. Hyenas. It sounded as if a pack of wild dogs were having sex with an unwilling monkey... and they were close.

The howling grew louder and yellow dots appeared from the darkness in pairs. The eyes floated in the air like fireflies, reflecting the light of the moon. He saw only a few pairs at first, but within seconds, the glowing dots surrounded them from all sides. The howling subsided, only to be replaced with a chorus of whines as the first of the pack came into view. The pattern of beige fur with black stripes looked similar to a zebra, but the mangy bodies were nowhere near as elegant. These animals had a hungry look in their eyes, their fur standing upright as they approached.

Athan grabbed Mara and boosted her to the top of the rock. He followed her up the side, but one step away from the top, he felt a pain shoot up through his leg. He looked down and saw a hyena attached to his ankle, its jaws clenched tight, digging into his flesh. Groaning in pain, he shook his leg, but the animal held tight. Swinging his leg out as far as he could, he knocked the hyena into the rock, causing it to lose its grip and fall back to the ground.

He finally reached the top and held his daughter close while nursing his injured leg, watching the blood trickle down his foot and into a small pool where they sat. He used a piece of his ripped shirt to wrap the wound and stem the bleeding. The hyenas made a few attempts to jump up the side of the rock, but it soon became clear that Athan and Mara sat out of their reach.

The hyenas circled the rock for hours, making a variety of cries. Athan wondered how long they would be trapped, but by morning the hyenas were gone. Before starting for the day, Athan looked at the horizon one last time for a clue as to which way they should travel. Still nothing in the distance, but the ground sloped up to a small peak to the north. Although the trek would be difficult, especially with no water, following the hill up would give them a new vantage point and their best chance of finding a settlement.

At this point, Athan noticed that during the night, the hyenas destroyed the last of their belongings. Sifting through the sand near where they slept, he became even more dejected when realizing that even their sandals were nowhere to be found. For now, the ground felt cool to the touch, but by mid-day, their feet would be on fire. Mara asked to be carried, but he told her to walk while she still could. He knew he would carry her before long. His calloused soles could hold up to the high temperature longer than her tender feet.

Mara walked quicker in the morning from the night's rest. The coolness of the sand between her toes livened her step, but it only took a few hours before her pace slowed. Athan's injured ankle appreciated the slower pace as the hill sloped up at a greater angle, and their legs began to ache.

"Just focus on putting one foot in front of the other. It's not much farther now," he said.

Anything to keep their minds away from the thirst. Their lips had cracked at the lack of water, but all they could do was push on. The sun had reached its highest point when they finally made it to the peak of the hill.

Sweat stung his eye as it dripped from Athan's brow. He wiped it away. Precious moisture that he could ill afford to lose. He had to stay strong for Mara.

This time Athan had prepared himself for the worst, expecting to see nothing but more sand as far as the eye could see. If they were lucky, they'd find shade to hide under for a while. That's why he became shocked to find a green patch of vegetation not too far off on the other side. Overcome with relief, Athan increased his pace, leaving his daughter behind. As he drew nearer, he couldn't believe his luck, spotting multiple acacia trees, a grassy patch, and what looked to be a small stream running down the middle!

Mara tried to keep up calling for her father, but he did not hear her calls. He continued running blindly towards the oasis, increasing his speed as he went until his legs became twisted in the sand under him, and he fell face first into the ground. This gave Mara a chance to catch up with him, but as he rose, a look of bewilderment crossed his face. He turned his head from side to side, looking for the oasis he had been running towards, but it was gone. Realizing he had been chasing a mirage, Athan was even more defeated than before. Still lying on the ground, he put his head down, face first into the sand, regardless of the burning sensation on his skin as he tried to hold back tears. He lay on the ground and pondered their fates as the heat from the sun beat down. They've had no water in over 24 hours. His older body might survive another day or two before giving out, but she needed hydration sooner. Thoughts of his daughter became the only thing that gave Athan the strength to stand and carry on. If not for her, he would be content to lie in the sand and wait for the end.

His shoulders, already burned from the previous day, felt raw as the sun beat down upon them. With no oasis in sight, Athan noted his surroundings again. This time, he saw a small shape on the horizon. Remembering his recent folly, he pointed the shape out to his daughter, who confirmed that she also saw something in the distance.

They began the trek with their new destination ahead. The flat path in front of them looked to be an easier walk than the hill they just climbed, but they soon remembered everything in the desert is harder than it seems. Rocks jutting out from the earth cut their feet as they walked, causing each step to be a struggle. The ground had now been sitting under the scorching desert sun all day and burned their soles as they walked. Their necks and shoulders continued to blister from the heat. Mara yelped in pain upon stepping on a hot patch and fell to her knees, burning herself even more as she did so.

She looked up at her father, her cheeks cracked and peeling from the hot dry air and said, "I can't go on."

"I know this is difficult, but we are being tested. We must persevere," Athan said as he ducked down, allowing her to climb onto his back.

Keeping his eyes trained on the object in the distance, he could have sworn it moved. Athan shook it off as another delusion, his mind clouded from the heat of the sun. The way the heat bounced off the desert floor in waves, everything seemed to be moving.

Athan prepared himself for another long hike but thankfully, they advanced upon this object rather quickly and, to his surprise, saw his eyes had been correct. A rather large ibex stood in front of them, neck lowered and hunched over, with two massive horns arching back from its head. Upon noticing them, the ibex stood upright and turned toward the pair. Face to face with the animal, Athan could see blood covering its mouth and neck. The fresh blood dripped down into the matted hair on its chest. The beast's fur was an unnatural burgundy color, stained with blood that had long since dried.

The animal locked eyes with Athan and he put Mara down. He advanced slowly, keeping his eyes trained on the ibex, whose own bloodshot eyes stayed fixed on Athan as well. Another step forward and the ibex let out a snort, baring its teeth. The menacing maw held teeth sharper than they should be for a natural herbivore. Living on farmland near the desert, Athan had become very familiar with the local ibex who often grazed in his fields. Their diet comprised only plants or grass from the surrounding areas. They never hunted other animals. He looked for the first time at the ground to the source of the meal and saw another ibex, blood spilling from a deep wound in its belly. The mortally injured creature's chest rose up and down as it gasped for breath. Athan did not know what to make of the sight in front of him. He now stood only a few steps from the two animals and the ibex had yet to run off, which it should have done at first sight of the humans.

Athan picked up a rock from the ground and threw it at the animal, letting out a "Hee-ya!" as he did. Startled by the impact of the rock, the ibex turned and ran, leaving only a dust cloud in its wake. Mara, cowering behind her father, peered around him to see the dying animal that lay before them. Athan ran his hand through his daughter's hair and let out a deep sigh. The tangy, sweet smell of blood had reached them both, causing their stomachs to growl in unison. After a day and a half in the desert with no food or water, he saw no other option. Crouching next to the ibex, Athan brought his mouth to the hole in its stomach and bit at the wound, hoping for any sort of sustenance. He closed his eyes and basked in the taste of the raw meat. As the ibex blood touched his tongue, an urge overcame Athan. He needed more. Putting his hand on animal's side, he pressed down firmly and the blood began flowing out. He caught what he could in his mouth, swallowing gulp after gulp of the warm liquid. Although a far cry from the water he so desperately needed, even the slightest moisture on his parched tongue felt like a drink of cool mead.

Suddenly remembering his daughter, he turned to find her wide eyed, looking horrified at seeing her father drink blood from the dying animal.

With a weary look, he said, "Mara, my girl, we have no other choice. Come and eat with me. We must survive at any cost."

Lost in the desert with the sun beating down, their skin blistered from the burns and their throat aching for a drop of moisture, Mara stood unfazed, slowly shaking her head from side to side.

The taste of the thick blood had soured on Athan's tongue, drying out even faster than it was moistened. The urge to force Mara to drink crossed his mind, but the hunger took over. Returning to the animal, he suckled the blood like a baby from its mother's teat, pressing harder on the animal to extract as much of the lifeblood as he could. As the flow slowed, Athan's hunger did not. He sunk his teeth into the animal and began gnawing on the exposed fat, tearing a larger opening with which to feed.

Mara stood over her father while he feasted upon the now dead animal. Her sun-blurred vision sparing her from the most gruesome details, but the cloying odor of blood and slurping sounds of her father's meal made her retch. Bending over to dry heave, she saw the pool of blood spreading around her father. Nothing would get her to eat from that animal, even if it meant her death.

Athan looked up again at his daughter, this time his hunger satiated enough for her to hold his attention. She could barely make eye contact with him, but he knew the sickly look on her face as she watched in horror. Tears streamed down Athan's cheeks as he realized just how low he had stooped. His only thought had been survival, but even if they made it out of the desert, would Mara ever look at him the same way again? If he died anyway, then he committed this deplorable act for nothing. His only hope was to be forgiven for his sins in the afterlife.

Athan felt the fresh blood coursing through his body. He sensed it channeling the endurance of the ibex, which gave him the strength to continue on. The nourishment would only last for so long and they still had to find shelter for the night. He wanted to avoid another run-in with the hyenas. Following the path of the ibex that ran off was the obvious choice. The animals knew the lay of the land, and hopefully, it would lead them to shelter or water.

Athan wiped his mouth on his forearm, doing little to clean the blood from his face but covering his arm in blood as well, and approached his daughter. Hesitating at the bloody man in front of her, she tentatively hopped on his back as he set off.

Her feverish body and bony fingers dug into his skin, but he was in a place beyond the point of pain. A primal feeling had taken over and Athan continued to trod through the sand, determined to survive. Mara grabbed at his arms as they walked, trying to keep hold, but his skin became sticky from the oozing blisters, causing her to lose her grasp repeatedly. As she clawed at his arms and back to stay on, the epidermis itself began tearing from his body. The only way to maintain her grip was by digging her fingers deep into his muscle tissue. Athan ignored it and continued on. The wind had picked up and visibility was low. Sand blew in their faces, making progress even tougher. Athan lowered his head and put one foot in front of the other. He walked like this for hours, feeling unnaturally strong, but the sun still burned his flesh and exposed muscle. By now, most of the skin from his back and arms hung off him in shredded tatters. Sand blew in their faces and stuck to the exposed pulpy flesh of Athan's back.

"Please Daddy, we must stop and rest," she begged as she struggled to maintain her grip on his slick back. Fluids that dripped from his torn skin now covered her entire body.

"Just a little farther, my dear. Hold tight and we'll find help soon." Athan began to second guess himself, wondering if following the direction of the ibex had been a bad idea. The animals weren't known to be very smart after all and this one, eating the flesh of its own... the beast must have been mad.

By now, Athan could feel the strength from his meal fading rapidly. He considered for the 100th time if he should just lie down and accept his fate. Just as these thoughts crossed his mind, the winds settled, expanding his vision. Off in the distance, he saw a shadow on the horizon. It looked almost like a dark set of eyes peering out of the sandstorm. Athan took it as a sign, from heaven or hell, he did not know or care. Yet, he adjusted his course and headed towards the shadowy structure.

As the visibility increased and Athan walked closer, it became clear that the eyes looking out at him were part of a large stone formation in a cliff. Up close, the rocks looked almost like a skull chiseled into the side of the bluff. The eyes of the skull bore deep into the rock, big enough for a person to crawl in. Shade. Athan increased his speed with a respite so close. Looking into the orifice, a shiver ran up his spine. Something about this cave gave him a strange feeling.

Finally arriving, he boosted Mara up into the opening. After she entered the inlet, Mara hesitated as a foul smell hit her senses. Athan forced her to press on, ignoring the odor, and climbed in after her. The openings were easily large enough for them to crawl through, and as luck would have it, the left eye went deep inside the cliff leading to a cave.

One step into the cavern and Athan collapsed in a heap on the floor. He had passed the physical limits of what his body could handle and felt a strange tingling sensation, almost as if he floated weightless through the air. Mara lay next to him, she too barely able to move from the lack of food and water. They had shade and shelter but would not last long without sustenance. Eventually Athan noticed the stale odor in the cave and raised his head to look around, an enormous effort in his current state. His eyes, still adjusting, couldn't make out much of his surroundings. With each breath, floating particles swirled through the air and into his lungs, leaving a taste of sulfur in his mouth. The particles let off a strange glow that gave the air a fog-like quality. His vision blurred, causing him to see double and triple. About to lose consciousness, he felt a strange sensation coming from his belly, still engorged with blood and raw meat. An itching burned his stomach and slowly stretched throughout his body. He could feel the mad ibex inside him. Then the realization came to him! They lay in the animal's home, and it would return soon, happy to find a free meal on its doorstep.

The ibex had only a single thought, a deep craving for blood. Athan didn't know how, but he felt connected to the beast in some way. He felt its desires inside of him, which caused his own hunger to return tenfold, like nothing he'd ever felt before. The hunger pains didn't seem to emanate from his stomach but from his entire body. His body ached for nourishment.

Unable to muster the strength to crawl back out, Athan and Mara would die in this cave. He turned his head to look at Mara's frail body. Her breathing slowed, and he knew she had little time left. He hated being helpless to save her, a father's only job, but he could help end her suffering. Surely that would be better than leaving her to waste away in pain? If she would die anyway, why let her precious blood go to waste? If she died, her blood would turn sour. He had to drink it now, while she still lived. He'd be doing her a favor, after all.

Grabbing hold of the floor, he pulled himself alongside his daughter and whispered in her ear, "Don't worry my precious girl, I will ease your pain." He leaned in, bit deeply into her soft neck and drank.

The Revenant

Wharram Percy, England
1217 AD

Roger Foley didn't believe in superstitions. He might've been the only soul in Wharram Percy without the fear of God in him. Instead of fearing God, he feared the wild beliefs of the other villagers. As far as religion is concerned, Roger couldn't care less about his neighbors' convictions and was wise enough not to debate it with them. He attended church regularly with the others, and whenever the topic of religion came up in discussion, he knew best to agree and move the conversation on to another topic. However, the denizens of Wharram Percy, a small farming town outside of York, had a monthly ritual that went far beyond any conventional religion's liturgy. But without proof, Roger put little faith in legend and had no plans to take part in their sick practice. The Foley family had been lucky so far and avoided selection during the town's ritual, but soon Roger would be of age to take part in the ceremony as well, and if he didn't do something, their luck wouldn't hold out forever.

The town's busybodies buzzed all morning, gossiping about the night's event, as they always did, on the day before the full moon. Preparations for the ritual were underway. The first of the villagers gathered around the town's only holding cell a few hours after noon. Still, a long time before sunset, they were eager to get on with the ceremony. The selection for this month's offering had been an easy one. A rare crime had been committed, which gave the villagers a sigh of relief that they would not have to draw names for the offering.

Finally, after hours of impatient waiting, the constable, Jed Grayson, made his way to the village jail cell. Holding a large metal key on a circular ring, he unlocked the door to retrieve the condemned. As the door cracked open, Jack Collins burst from the cell, making a break for freedom. Jed, being an older gentleman, well past his prime and having been through this before, came prepared with backup. One large man waited on each side of the building, bludgeon in hand, waiting to strike if needed. As Jack ran by, the man closest to him swung his weapon, striking Jack in the leg with a crunching sound. Jack yelped in pain and fell to the ground, clutching his bruised shin. The two men grabbed the convict under his arms, yanking him to his feet. The sun sank in the sky, inching closer to the horizon. There was no time for delays.

"Please... spare me, I beg of you," Jack mumbled as the men dragged him down the path leading out of town. "Surely you wouldn't condemn a man to die for such a petty crime as stealing something to eat."

"You knew the rules of this town and broke them anyway," the constable replied.

As customary, the people of the village walked with the condemned out of town to a clearing in the woods. Jack limped on his injured leg, but his captors forced him to keep a brisk pace. Upon reaching the clearing, a large wooden post came into view. The post emerged from the ground in the center of the clearing. Attached to the post lay a chain, which the constable fastened to the prisoner's ankle. Dejected and realizing his pleas for mercy fell on deaf ears, Jack gave up begging for his freedom and struggled no longer. If they were to free his bonds, someone would need to take his place, and for that, there would be no volunteers.

The sun, disappearing under the horizon, caused the trees to leave long shadows that stretched through the clearing. Beams of pink light gleamed between the trunks as the sun crept lower. The Revenant would arrive soon and the legend said anyone who dared look upon the creature while it fed, would be cursed to share the fate of the damned. With a warning as ominous as that, no one stayed behind to watch.

The crowd formed a circle around the post, with only the constable remaining in the center, along with Jack, who had sat down to nurse his wounded leg. He rolled up his trousers to expose a gnarly bruise from the bludgeon strike. Beads of blood dripped down to his ankle, leaving a stain on his stocking.

The constable took a step forward and cleared his throat. The murmuring of the crowd came to a hush, and he began, "People of Wharram Percy, we all know the reason for our congregation today. We are here to honor the agreement our ancestors made with the Revenant. This sacrifice weighs heavy on our hearts, but we will persevere. Please remember, this pact is the only reason any of us are still alive. Even though this man is here today because of the crime he committed, his name will go into our record books as a hero and savior of this town. We thank you, Jack Collins, for your ultimate sacrifice."

Roger stood with his parents as he listened to the speech, eyes trained on the hopeless prisoner. He felt sorry for the poor man. The legend of the Revenant is a hundred years old. No one alive in town has set eyes upon the creature, yet they still do its bidding and sacrifice one of their own each month to the so-called monster in the woods.

Roger mused about the holes in the villagers' lore. *Leaving a man tied to a post in the middle of the forest. Of course, he will wind up dead the next morning. Between the bears, wolves and other animals that prowled these woods, something would surely come for a helpless meal.*

With the constable's speech finished, the villagers wandered back down the trail, eager to get back to the safety of the town walls. Roger stood in the clearing, looking at the man tied to the post, when a grand idea came to him. He could free the man and prove once and for all the legend is false, thus sparing future sacrifices and becoming the true hero of Wharram Percy. Sure, they might be angry at first, but after realizing their foolish obedience to a myth, they would hail Roger as a savior.

Roger snapped out of his daydream as his father called his name to hurry along. He took one last glance at Jack, who sat on the dusty ground to await his fate. Their eyes locked for a moment before Roger turned to walk away with his family.

On the way back to town, Roger's parents struck up a conversation with another man and right before they entered the gate, Roger took his chance to slip off into the woods. He hoped no one noticed his sudden disappearance, but he dared not glance behind him.

Roger circled back to the clearing, keeping off the path to stay hidden from any stray villagers. He ducked behind a large tree and some bushes on the outskirts of the clearing to remain out of sight. He looked again at the man chained to a pole and left outside to die alone in the woods. Roger considered his options. A few strikes from a sharp rock should break the rusted chain, and he could free Jack. If his family wouldn't listen to the obvious truth, he'd leave this place behind and go without them, taking Jack as a companion.

On Roger's next birthday, the townspeople will include him in the ritual, increasing his family's chance of being selected for the offering. Petrified of this horrible fate, Roger constantly begged his parents to pack up their belongings and leave this ill-fated town. His father always refused, citing the original pact made with the other families ages ago.

According to the town's legend, an undying man who feasts on human flesh stalked the forest at night and has done so for hundreds of years. The Revenant, as he came to be called, lured children deep into the forest. They always found the poor children the next day, pale as ghosts, their faces frozen in terror. For an unknown reason, the younglings wandered into the forest, one by one, in the middle of the night. No one knew why, so the villagers locked the children up at night and kept them under watch. With the children unable to escape during the night, adults went missing instead. Slipping out of bed, they wandered off into the woods the same as the children had done. The town increased the number of patrols and eventually one spotted a young lady walking out of camp on her own one night. The young madam still wore her dressing gown and drifted along in a trance as if she were sleepwalking. A few men gathered to follow her into the woods and watched her meet the vile monster. This repulsive beast looked to be a feral human with white skin and long teeth. The monster took hold of her and bit deeply into her neck, drinking blood straight from her vein. The woman made no effort to resist; instead, it seemed as if she offered herself to the foul thing, even moaning in pleasure as it fed from her. After seeing this horrible sight, the men confronted the monster, hoping to catch it off guard while it fed, but the men underestimated the beast.

The Revenant knew it was being watched, and was ready when the men emerged from their position. Although the Revenant outclassed them and could easily dispatch the entire group, he had weaknesses of his own and had no interest in an all out war with the colony. He preferred to stay underground in his lair, safe from the deadly sunlight, emerging from his slumber only when necessary to feed. Having to lure victims from the town took a heavy toll on his psyche and required more frequent feeding. So the Revenant spoke to the villagers, not with words, but directly through their minds, and explained his situation. He was only doing what was required for him to survive. The children's young minds had been easier to enchant but if the town delivers him a monthly tribute, their children could rest safe once again. Without the need to hunt, the Revenant could hibernate longer, needing to feed less often, and only arise once a month on the full moon. The villagers agreed. They would leave a sacrifice, ensuring another month of safety for the rest.

This is how the people of Wharram Percy came to an understanding with the monster. Instead of luring people from their homes, the villagers left an offering on each full moon. The townsfolk agreed to the deal and decided sending the town criminals to their death seemed a better option than the deaths of their children and wives. However, the Revenant gave one last warning before disappearing into its lair. If the villagers ever broke the pact or interfered with his feeding, they would pay a steep price.

At first glance, the agreement seemed like a win-win. With the curfew lifted, life returned to normal in the small village. The monster in the forest remained satiated while criminals met a gruesome end. However, soon enough, fear of being fed to the beast caused crime to drop in Wharram Percy and, after a while, they ran out of criminals to offer as tribute. This required the people to develop a new method of selecting the sacrifice. Every soul in town, over the age of seventeen, would place his name on a rock. Each month, if no criminals awaited their execution, the priest picked one rock from a barrel to be chosen as an offering. If the priest selected a young soul from the barrel, an elder family member could volunteer to take his place. The people honored those who were sacrificed, inscribing their names in the town temple. They became revered by all who lived there. Rarely did one of the chosen put up a fight. Most viewed it as an honorable death for the good of the village.

Roger considered his options. They shouldn't condemn this man to death for stealing a loaf of bread. If he freed the prisoner, he could prove to the village, once and for all, the legend is false. On the other hand, if the man escapes and the legend turns out to be true, he would damn his parents to the wrath of the Revenant. Roger didn't care about the other villagers, but even though he resented his parents for forcing him to stay in this awful town, he couldn't take a chance of causing them harm.

The battle raged in Roger's head, and a hush came over the forest. The birds and crickets grew silent and the sounds of leaves rustling in the distance ceased. It seemed as if even the wind came to a halt. The hairs in Roger's nose tingled as he noticed a subtle change in the air. Seeming to come out of nowhere, a thick fog descended upon the clearing, reducing Roger's visibility. He saw the shadow of Jack Collins, kneeling on the ground, tied to the post in the center of the clearing. Anything beyond was a haze.

As the fog thickened, a different type of fog clouded Roger's thoughts. For a moment, he forgot what he was doing. *Why was he hunkered down behind a tree in the woods?* Then he saw another form appear in the mist. A tall, slender humanoid shadow. Roger couldn't make out anything other than a few blurry shapes, because of his obscured vision, but as the man's form solidified, the mist faded. The only sound came from Jack, who crawled away backwards as far as his chain allowed. He whimpered an inaudible prayer as the strange being approached.

The shadow man leaned over Jack and their forms became one as Jack let out a sharp cry and then nothing. His whimpers ceased. Roger couldn't believe his eyes. *Could the legend actually be true? Surely this must be an outcast who, in his desperation for food, sunk to cannibalism. That makes more sense than a true undead revenant.* Either way, Roger already regretted his decision to return to the clearing and didn't care to stick around and find out who the man really was. Still hidden behind the brush, he looked around to determine the best route of retreat when a booming voice called out.

"Do not be afraid, boy. You must be curious. I don't blame you. Come into the moonlight, so we can see each other properly."

The voice rang in Roger's head, but didn't seem to come from the direction of the strange figure. Still, the man stood and looked in Roger's direction. Roger saw him clearly now that the fog had lifted. The thing before him looked like an unnaturally tall human with tattered clothes and pale skin except for large dark circles around his eyes and crimson red lips.

Before Roger knew what he was doing, he stood and walked out from behind the tree. As Roger stepped into the open and came closer to the Revenant, the creature's prominent features became clear. His sunken eyes contained huge pupils of pure darkness so black they looked like empty sockets. The surrounding sclera, a hue of dark pink instead of white.

As Roger neared the center of the clearing, what he took for the Revenant's clothes were not clothes at all but layers of dirt. For the first time, Roger noticed the thing before him was completely naked. Centuries of grime encrusted the creases of the creature's wrinkled skin, concealing his nakedness and giving his body a darker shade than the anemic look of his face.

Again Roger heard the same voice, "Come closer, my boy, I will not hurt you."

Roger was certain the voice came from the tall man in front of him, but he had been looking directly at him and the man's mouth remained closed. His bright red lips were motionless, except for a drop of blood that glistened as it rolled down his chin.

Roger was repulsed by the Revenant, but found himself putting one foot in front of the other until he stood face to face with it. He looked down at Jack, dying on the ground with blood turning the dry dirt into a muddy puddle of death. A few moments ago, he felt such empathy for this man. Now, with indifference, he returned his gaze to the Revenant.

Suddenly, something broke the Revenant's hold on him and Roger's mind snapped back to reality. Realization of his imminent peril came over him and he panicked. His thoughts went to his parents, and he wondered if his mother had noticed his disappearance yet. But just as quick as the memory came over him, it faded, and he returned to the grip of the Revenant's seduction, forgetting any cause for alarm.

"Who are you?" Roger asked the thing in front of him.

"I go by many names, but you know who I am. Ask your true question, boy." he answered, mouth still unmoving.

"What are you?"

"I am a Revenant. The undying. I am cursed to walk the Earth until the end of time, feeding on the blood of my own kind."

The Revenant looked directly at Roger, face remaining stoic, and opened his arms as if expecting an embrace. Barely more than skin and bones, the outline of each rib protruded from his chest. Roger stepped even closer, putting his cheek against the bony bumps on the man's abdomen. Roger nuzzled the Revenant's decaying flesh as a baby animal cuddles against its mother. The Revenant placed one arm around Roger, holding him close and shuddering at the warmth of the human. Its other hand extended in the air, showing off its long, pointed fingernails that were caked with soot and discolored with swirls of yellow and gray. The Revenant brought its hand to its own chest with a single finger extended. The creature's discolored nail pierced the skin just below its withered nipple and dug deeply into the flesh. It dragged its finger, tearing a fissure in the gray skin. Thick blood trickled from the wound and rolled down its chest, coming to a rest on Roger's lips. As it did, his mouth cracked open with a barely audible moan escaping from his throat. As more blood came down and pooled around Roger's lips, his tongue emerged, lapping at the decrepit man's skin. He took up blood and dirt together in his mouth. His lips puckered at the sour flavor of the mixture as it coursed through his taste buds. More blood came out of the Revenant's upper rib, rolling down his chest. Roger, with his tongue slowly dancing along the rotten flesh, raised himself up, scooping the droplets of blood up into his mouth and down his throat. The cold skin of the Revenant contrasted with the warmth of its sticky blood. Roger followed the trail of blood with his tongue until he reached the source. A dark red fluid oozed from the wound like a thick sap. The blood Roger lapped up was so dark, it looked black in the moonlight. He suckled directly on the gash, his mouth open, tongue moving in and out as if passionately kissing a lover. Roger's eyes closed in ecstasy, thinking of nothing but the pleasure from each drop of blood that touched his lips, when suddenly the arm that so lovingly embraced him tore him away from the source of the nectar.

"Enough," said the man in front of him. "Now, go."

At first, he was confused and angry at being ripped from the blood and wanted more. Roger quickly became horrified at the realization of his actions. He fell backwards to the ground in disgust. His body wanted to wretch at the repugnant fluids swimming in his belly, but his mind told him he needed more.

"Go!" said the Revenant again, louder this time.

Ready to run, but knowing this could be his last chance for more answers, he dared one last question. "Why let me live? According to the legend of our agreement, anyone who looks on you would share his fate," Roger asked as he motioned at Jack, who lay on the ground, shivering in a state of unconsciousness and turning blue from the loss of blood at his neck.

The Revenant smiled at the mistake. For the first time, the human-like monster opened his mouth, and a laugh escaped his throat, showing off his sharpened canine teeth. "You have misinterpreted the agreement. You are not to share the fate of the dead, but the fate of the damned."

Roger, still unsure of the Revenant's meaning, regained his wits and continued backing away. The Revenant, still emitting a strange laughter, returned to finish his meal before too much of the precious red liquid went to waste. Roger turned and ran off as fast as his legs would carry him down the trail back towards his village, subconsciously licking his lips, hoping to taste any of the foul blood that remained.

Upon seeing his approach, the watchman on duty called out, stirring up a commotion on the other side of the gate. By the time Roger reached the barrier, the guards had cracked it open to let him inside before hastily securing it as soon as the boy stepped through.

Roger found himself surrounded by men who seemed not sure what to make of his late arrival on the night of the full moon. Some had their weapons drawn, ready to strike. Roger's mother, who had been searching for her missing son, pushed through the crowd to her boy's side.

"Put your weapons away. He is just a boy. He came back in time. If he didn't, he would have never made it back at all," she pleaded as she looked between the men, meeting each of their eyes.

The men looked at each other, unsure of what to do. Apprehensively, they parted, allowing Roger to return home with his parents. With nothing more to see, the crowd dispersed and went on their way.

Back in the privacy of their home, a family argument ensued. Roger saw the look of rage on his father's face, but he needed to make one last attempt to convince his family to flee. "Please Dad, there is still time. We can leave together right now and by the time we are missed, we'll be on the road to a new city," Roger begged his father.

His father glared back with a stone-faced look and unleashed his fury at the boy's deception. "Are you insane? First, you know I would never abandon this village and second, we would never get by the guards. You have embarrassed this family enough already!"

He dragged Roger to his room, knocking into furniture along the way. Upon entering, he threw Roger to the floor, raised his hand as if to strike, and said, "Do you think this is a joke? We have put up with your insolence for too long. You are lucky you came back in time. Starting tomorrow, things will change around here. It is time you learned some discipline!"

With that, he slammed the door and left Roger to his tears. So much had happened to him in the past hour that he barely had time to process all of it. His dad's anger, the villager's fear, his mother's unconditional love, but one thought returned to his mind over and over. The sour taste of the Revenant's blood. Roger made his way to his bed and crawled under the covers, turning them into a cocoon. Within minutes, he fell into a trance-like sleep, shaking and murmuring while he dozed.

That night, in Roger's dreams, he saw colors. Dark tones that melted and swirled, pooling into each other like buckets of paint, mixing to create new shades. He sank in the thick liquid, flailing his arms in an attempt to keep his head above the surface. As he struggled, his arms and legs became heavy in the viscous fluid, weighing him down as if swimming in cement.

While Roger underwent his transformation, the other inhabitants of Wharram Percy had their own visions. In these vivid dreams, virtually identical for all the townsfolk, the Revenant visited them and called to stir them from their slumber. His pale, naked form appeared in their minds and beckoned them out of their homes. Like clockwork, everyone emerged from their houses, unsure why they had awoken or what pulled them from their beds.

A voice boomed from everywhere and nowhere all at once. "The pact has been broken. The boy will return with me after he feeds."

The crowd looked for the source of the voice, unsure from which direction it came. Many cowered and wished to scurry back inside their homes but could not break the paralysis. The constable took it upon himself to reply, asking, "H-Hello? Who is this? What boy? What are you talking about?"

The voice boomed again, echoing inside the villagers' skulls, causing many to double over in pain or massage their head to ease the ache. "Don't play coy! The boy has looked upon me during my feeding and now, he will be as I am, cursed to walk the earth for eternity."

"Sir!" said one of the gatehouse guards. "The Foley boy. He came in after sunset."

At that moment, the door to Roger's house burst open. His mother emerged screaming, "Help! Help! Someone. He's gone mad!"

Roger followed her from the house, his clothes soaked in blood. The snarl on his face exposed one of his newly formed fangs. Pieces of his father remained stuck between his teeth as he searched for more blood to quench his growing hunger.

Two guards raised their bows to unleash a volley on Roger, but as they released their arrows, a swarm of bats descended from nowhere, obscuring the target. The arrows fell, each with a bat skewered on their flight, still twitching as they hit the ground. The swarm flocked to the archers, preventing them from firing again. Two other men drew their swords and closed in on Roger.

By this time, the Revenant had commanded the guards to open the gate. He stood outside the gate and watched the chaos unfold. Already weary from spending his mental stamina waking the entire village, he called on his powers once more. His voice resonated in the villagers' head again, commanding them to stop. Roger also felt the draw of his creator and followed the call through the gate.

Watching Roger's escape, the villagers noticed the naked man standing outside for the first time. Although clearly the same man Roger had met earlier and still coated in layers of filth, he looked decades younger and healthier. Having enjoyed his first meal in thirty days, the undead man's physical strength and complexion returned. Roger took his place next to his creator and looked back at the frightened people whom he once called his neighbors.

He stood just outside the town walls and watched the terrified villagers. The Revenant spoke, this time using his mouth as if he were nothing more than an average man. "We seal this new arrangement with everyone who stands before me as a witness. There are now two of us. We will require two offerings every full moon."

The constable was quick to reply, "W-We can't afford to sacrifice two every month. We can barely get by as it is. Soon enough, there'll be none of us left. And that means nothing for you either."

"That is your problem. What would you have me do? We need to eat. Should I unleash my new protégé to hunt in these forests unabated?" He turned to his companion. "Would you like that, my boy? Free roam of these woods."

The constable replied, "F-Fine. Whatever you say. We'll do it. It's not like we have a choice."

"Then it is agreed," replied the Revenant.

In a newly descending haze of fog, the two undead souls faded from view, but not before one last warning from the monster. "Don't think you can betray our deal by fleeing. You are all marked, and if you run, there is nowhere we can't find you." With that, they disappeared into the darkness.

The villagers were left alone to ponder their fate. Most stood in quiet disbelief. The sounds of Miss Foley's sobs resonated across the town. With everyone already present, a meeting was held. The villagers knew their small town could never sustain sacrificing two people each month. Some wanted to flee regardless of the warning, but more refused to abandon their family homestead. By way of a vote, the townspeople made their decision. They had thirty days to prepare for their next encounter with the revenants. They would make no more offerings to the monsters.

The Vampire of Notre-Dame

P aris, France
1482

The sixth of January, 1482, is not a day of which history has preserved the memory, however the following is the true account of what transpired on that fateful day and those that preceded it.

Two hours before dawn and the streets still covered in darkness, the bells of the Notre-Dame Cathedral rang loudly across Paris. Crowds had already filled the main square in front of the most magnificent cathedral in all of France. Throngs of people, mostly commoners and peasants, overflowed the square and spilled onto the adjacent streets. They were there at this early hour to see an execution. The early morning announcement made no mention of who was to be hung, but everyone vied for a spot to glimpse the lynching.

Rumors had swirled throughout the city of a monster that lives in the bell tower and stalks the streets at night. The villagers had long debated whether the one who lived in the tower was a man or a beast, and they made many a wager as to its true nature. There were those who refused to believe in the supernatural no matter how much evidence existed, and others who had seen glimpses of a creature that exhibited speed and agility far greater than that of an average human.

The gallows had been a permanent fixture in the square since Archdeacon Claude Frollo had taken charge of the Notre-Dame. Having a very close relationship with the king, the church advised the throne on all matters, including carrying out punishments for lawbreakers. Due to the growing influence of the church on the crown, hangings were scheduled weekly for criminals and blasphemers, of which there were many. They announced supplemental executions as needed, such as this one, by the ringing of the eight bells in Notre-Dame's north tower.

The cathedral loomed over the square with its enormous dual towers. Saints and gargoyles alike were chiseled into the exterior of the building to honor and protect the holy place. Construction for the magnificent cathedral, which began in 1163, took 182 years to complete with over a thousand laborers toiling on it.

From the top of the tower, Quasimodo intently watched the scene below. He lived in the rafters of the bell tower, at the behest of Archdeacon Frollo, hidden away from the masses on the streets. Frequently, the people below had heard the cries from the tower and seen shadows dance in the moonlight, causing speculation as to what manner of beast lived inside. If the revelers on the streets below laid eyes on Quasimodo, they would be horrified by the distorted figure before them, but this has not always been the case.

Once, a long time ago, Quasimodo was a normal boy just like any other. A fit and carefree young man, strolling home with his well-to-do bourgeoisie parents on the cobblestone streets of Paris. One night, on the way home from a show, a strange man stopped them in the street. Although Quasimodo remembered little from that night, both of his parents died in what the authorities blamed on a random mugging. Quasimodo was never the same after that night, but the changes that occurred were physical as well as emotional. Only flashes of that night came to him in his dreams, as he suppressed the worst of the killings and never put two and two together until later. Instead, he considered himself fortunate to be found and taken in by Monseigneur Claude Frollo that same night.

Claude lived a lonely life as archdeacon of the famed Notre-Dame Cathedral. Although he had plenty of clergy and parishioners to keep him company, his true nature kept him from being able to confide in any of them. He could not have children of his own, but not for the reason priests don't have children. Claude had a dark secret and needed a loyal companion to confide in, to help keep his madness at bay.

The lessons Claude had for his new protégé did not go according to his plan. The transition to vampire on the same night of losing his parents was more than Quasimodo could handle at such a young age.

Upon learning that it was his new master who had ripped his old life away and given him this thirst for blood, Quasimodo rebelled against his creator by refusing his trainings. As tenants of the Notre-Dame and respected members of the clergy, there were multitudes of nameless beggars to feast on whose disappearance would go unnoticed. This unfettered access to the poor was one of the main reasons Claude had taken the job at the church. Plus, there was something amusing about hiding in plain sight alongside the ones who despise you. The Archdeacon brought many victims for Quasimodo to feed upon. However, his hate for the man who killed his parents outweighed his new thirst for blood. Thus, he refused to feed on humans and take any more lives. Claude Frollo became mad with rage over his protégé's refusal to feed and give in to his true nature. In this refusal, Quasimodo denied Frollo of his much sought vampire companion. Claude, being the older and stronger vampire, overpowered Quasimodo and locked him in the bell tower, offering only to release him only when Quasimodo was ready to feed as a vampire should.

Quasimodo spent years in the bell tower, locked away, unable as well as unwilling to feed on the human blood that his body now required. Although he received occasional visits from his creator, Quasimodo's loneliness in the years that followed grew so immense that he lost his sanity, speaking instead with the bells themselves and even naming them. They spoke to him every hour when the dual bells in the south tower rang out. The eight bells in the north tower rang often as well to signify various religious or political occasions. So loud was the ringing that any human who lived in the tower would have lost his hearing long ago. The immortal ears of a vampire, however, in addition to being a hundred times more sensitive than a human's, would heal themselves just as quickly as they ruptured. The result being the worst case of tinnitus the world has ever known. Quasimodo's ears would ring so loudly during moments of silence, his only peace occurred when the bells of Notre-Dame rang louder than the bells inside his head.

Along with the improved hearing came improved sight, and that was a heightened sense Quasimodo was glad for. He passed his time watching the citizens on the streets below as an eagle watches the mice from the skies. There were markets with vendors selling fresh meats, cheeses, breads and other food, as well as artisans with paintings of famous sights or serene landscapes. Beggars and pickpockets littered the square as prominent figures scurried through, often escorted by soldiers or bodyguards. One sight in the square that Quasimodo looked forward to more than any other, that of the beautiful Esmerelda. She danced in the square for coins and made quite the sum during the day. Her outfits, made of brightly colored silks or linens in every color of the rainbow, often with shoulders or even midriff exposed, dazzled the onlookers in the square. Some called her a gypsy, street trash or a whore, but to Quasimodo... she was nothing short of an angel.

Alone in the tower, with no pulse of his own, his skin cold to the touch, Quasimodo yearned to feel her warm flesh. He hung his head in sorrow at the simple pleasures in life that he would never know. With the deformities that plagued his body growing slightly larger and more misshapen every day, he knew one look at him would cause her to run in fear and repulsion.

With no humans to feed on, Quasimodo had no choice but to eat the rodents that scurried along the corners of the tower, along with any birds who landed within his walls. Vampires however, were not meant to live off the blood of lesser animals. To continue any semblance of a normal existence, they require blood from the species they originated as. Over the years that followed, Quasimodo continued to refuse the offerings his creator brought him, causing Frollo to trek up the winding stairs less and less often. On those infrequent occasions, Quasimodo stayed hunched in a corner or clung to the eaves, refusing to even look at his master. On one of Frollo's visits, however, he glimpsed something on Quasimodo's chin and suddenly saw a striking difference in his failed pupil. The change began so subtly; it went unnoticed until something as simple as a string of drool brought his attention to the right spot. Yanking Quasimodo out of the shadows, the full extent of his disfigurement came into view. This was not the usual change that happens when a human turns into a vampire; that metamorphosis had long since been complete.

The lesser animals that Quasimodo fed on catalyzed the transformation. Frollo had heard tales of feral vampires who became deformed over time because of the animals they fed upon, but this is the first time he'd seen it firsthand. Quasimodo's jaw had become elongated and his mouth protruded, almost like a snout. Frollo pulled Quasimodo close to inspect the monstrosity before him, but Quasimodo ripped himself away. As the disfigured vampire retreated to his corner, his stature seemed smaller, as if he were walking in a crouch. His whole form had become twisted and disfigured, tufts of hair protruding from moles growing on his body. It was almost as if, with every drop of blood that went into his gullet, Quasimodo gained characteristics of the animals that he fed upon.

That is when Claude decided enough was enough. He would not stand by any longer and let this pitiful excuse for a vampire go on in this manner. Claude turned to Quasimodo and said, "I have seen how you watch the gypsy girl who dances in the square. Esmerelda is it? You think I haven't seen the way you leer at her? Tonight, you will come with me and feast your carnal desires upon her!"

The deformed vampire, not wanting to kill the woman he yearned for, but eager for an opportunity to leave the tower and walk the streets once again, knew there was no point in arguing with the stronger vampire. Even glimpsing the magnificent halls of the cathedral would be a welcome change compared to his tired surroundings in the tower. Quasimodo reluctantly followed his master through the church's great hall. On his way out of the cathedral, he marveled at the magnificent rows of limestone pillars, grand archways, the intricate stained glass windows and granite steps leading up to the altar.

Outside in the alleyways of Paris, a light rain came down from the night sky, the moon almost but not quite full. Its light shone through the clouds that moved across the sky at a rapid pace, pushed along by a steady wind. Quasimodo lurched in the shadows, not moving for fear of being spotted, but Frollo pushed him along, unconcerned with the passersby. He was used to being in public, and although Quasimodo's deformed body would surely attract a few stares, there were enough freaks roaming the streets that the attention he attracted would quickly move on to the next oddity that caught their eye.

Street after street flashed by as Frollo dragged Quasimodo through the alleyways. Before he knew it, they had come to a stop and there, standing before them, was the breathtakingly beautiful Esmerelda. Almost finished packing her belongings to head home for the night, she spotted the pair approaching and turned toward them. Never being this close to her before, Quasimodo stood in awe, taken aback by her beauty. Her supple skin was free of blemishes and the curls of her ebony hair shone in the moonlight. This was the first time Quasimodo had been close enough to smell the sweetness of her flesh. He inhaled deeply, taking the pheromones deep into his lungs when their eyes locked and he could see a look of pity across her face. Pity for the deformed wretch that stood before her. If she only knew that his ugliness on the outside did not reflect his beauty on the inside. How he gave up any semblance of a normal life by refusing to kill his fellow man. He would always think of himself as a man, even if at this point he was far removed from anything close to human.

Quasimodo backed away, his emotions conflicting with his natural instincts. He knew this would be his only chance to touch her... to taste her. He knew from the look upon her face that she would never willingly be with a monster such as him.

Frollo sensed the battle going on inside Quasimodo's head and knew this was his chance. He grabbed her by the arm and pulled her roughly toward Quasimodo exposing the tender flesh of her wrist. He extended a finger and dug the sharp tip of his long nail into her wrist. A stream of blood spilled from the cut, dripping down her arm and spilling onto the ground.

"Now my child, you can taste the beauty that you so desire. Come and drink from her sweet veins."

The look on Esmerelda's face turned from pity to horror. However, Quasimodo resisted the temptation of blood and the archdeacon's voice had the opposite of its intended effect. Quasimodo's resolve hardened as he started shaking his head and continued to back away. "I won't do it!" he groaned.

"Fine, have it your way then. I'll have her myself," Claude replied as he opened his mouth revealing his protruding fangs.

Seeing his beloved in danger, something in Quasimodo snapped. He felt all the hate for his master that had been building up over the years and jumped towards Frollo with a single leap landing directly on top of him and catching the older vampire by surprise. Frollo released his grip on Esmerelda who stood still, stricken with shock by the events unfolding in front of her.

Quasimodo, eyes still fixed on Esmerelda, yelled for her to run. This snapped her out of the trance and her legs began moving. Quasimodo may have started the fight with the upper hand, but Frollo, being significantly older and stronger, quickly turned the tables. By then, however, the girl was gone, infuriating Frollo even more. He thought about ending Quasimodo right there, and even though he despised this thing his child had become, deep down he still had paternal feelings towards him. He was, after all, the only vampire he ever created. Instead, Frollo bounded off back to the cathedral with his ugly pet in tow before catching any unwanted attention.

Back at his tower and locked away again, Quasimodo felt helpless to aid his love. He knew Frollo would never allow Emerelda to live with the knowledge of his true nature that she now possessed. Her only hope would be to convince the authorities to act before the vampire Frollo found her, but persuading anyone that such a respected figure in the community was a monster would be no simple task.

Lost in the thoughts swirling inside his head, the bells in the north tower suddenly rang out. Quasimodo knew the ringing of the bells at this odd hour before dawn signaled only one thing. A coming execution. But who could it be? It had only been a few hours since the attack. Surely they wouldn't have moved against the archdeacon that quickly. However, if he was found out to be a vampire, they would no doubt act with haste to dispatch him.

The crowd that had quickly gathered came to a hush as the cathedral gates opened. Quasimodo strained to see who emerged, but from his vantage point in the tower above, his efforts were useless. He could do nothing but wait.

Eventually, the procession came into view. Two soldiers led the way in full uniform, followed by the hangman, a tall slender man with a long mustache, wearing a black doublet with gray hose. Although the next person's face was out of view, the flowing black robes with bells jingling from the seams were easily recognizable as Archdeacon Claude Frollo. To Quasimodo's dismay, he walked with his usual stature and did not appear to be bound or under duress in any way. Quasimodo's attention turned to the soldier following Frollo who held a rope that led to the bound arms of a hooded figure. The hood did nothing to obscure the identity of the condemned from Quasimodo. Curls of black hair flowed out from under the hood, leading to a red and white ruffled dress with exposed arms the perfect shade of olive.

As the Archdeacon approached the podium, the crowd grew quiet once again. "People of Paris! After a thorough investigation by our king's guard, it has been determined that the rumors and sightings of a monster lurking in our streets and preying upon the weak have been nothing but a trick. A sleight of hand to instill fear in the people of this city and then using that fear to rob us blind! We have all been under the influence of a witch who goes by the name of Esmeralda! As she danced in this very square, she conspired with demons against us!" As he finished his speech, Frollo yanked the hood off the woman and the crowd erupted in jeers.

The hangman, standing behind Esmerelda, affixed the noose around her neck. She struggled against the guard who gripped her with both hands and tried to say something, but her mouth had been gagged and no words would come out. Quasimodo knew her words without needing to hear them but her attempt at unmasking the real monster before the crowd would prove futile.

Everything that Quasimodo has suffered mentally and physically will be for nothing if they hung Esmerelda a witch. He needed to do something! He grabbed a rope and leaped from the tower, propelling down the stone facade. After climbing down as far as the rope would allow, Quasimodo was still too high to jump, even for a vampire. He stepped down onto a ledge, which gave way as he put his full weight upon it. He descended quickly, leaping from perch to perch, putting large gashes with his claws in the building's side as he went. At this point, some of the crowd had noticed and were pointing during his descent. After he'd covered about half the distance, Quasimodo landed on a stone gargoyle that lined the church's exterior and leaped the rest of the way down to the street below. He landed with a thud, cracking the stones below his feet and startling the nearby onlookers. He dashed through the crowd towards the gallows, ready to tear through anyone who tried to prevent him from reaching his beloved, but to his surprise, the way was clear. Quasimodo jumped up onto the platform, which was now empty except for Esmerelda. The guards and other men had backed away at the first sight of Quasimodo's approach. He could feel the thousands of eyes on him as he climbed to the top of the gallows and with a swipe of his claws, cut the rope suspending Esmerelda in the air, dropping her to the wooden platform below.

Quasimodo dropped next to her, but her face had turned a deep shade of purple, and her chest made no movements. He was too late, Esmerleda was dead. Quasimodo could feel the anger building inside him and spun around looking for the one who did this, but

Claude Frollo had used the distraction to slip away into the crowd. Now it seemed the soldiers had found their courage and were closing in around the stage with various spears and crossbows all trained at Quasimodo. With Claude nowhere in sight, Quasimodo's anger subsided, and sadness for Esmerelda overcame him. Turning back to her, he hobbled close and put his arms around her corpse as he curled up next to her and a tear streamed down his cheek. With the vampire's attention elsewhere, the soldiers had climbed back on the platform and poised to strike. Quasimodo did not care what the soldiers did to him as long as he held his love in this embrace. He touched her flesh gently. Her warmth radiated through his icy touch. Before the soldiers reached him, the first rays of the morning sun peeked over the horizon, instantly searing Quasimodo's skin. His flesh sizzled and blistered, resembling bacon frying on a griddle albeit with a putrid smell. Within a few seconds, he had been reduced to nothing more than ash and bone, leaving a decayed skeleton embracing the corpse of a witch, beautiful even in death. Later, when they tried to detach the skeleton which held her in his embrace, he fell to dust.

The Lonely Road

I nterstate 70, USA
1968

I guess it's time for a proper introduction. My real name's Gene McGrath and, as you can see, I'm on the road, rolling down the interstate. It feels like I'm always on the road, but that's the job. I hope you like music; it helps pass the time. I prefer rock 'n roll, but am open to suggestions. Hell, with the amount of driving I do, I can listen to every station on the dial until they play the same songs over again. Criss-crossing back and forth around the country from one state to the next, sometimes only to turn right around and head back the way I came is par for the course. This is the life of a hunter, heading whichever way the wind blows. After a while, these stretches of highway all look the same. I'm not even sure if we're in Indiana or Illinois. Does it even really matter?

Looks like that sign says Marshall, Illinois. Not as far along as I'd hoped, still another five hours to go. I'm gonna' pull off here for a pit stop. Got to fill up the car's tank and drain mine. Call it déjà vu or psychic intuition, but I think there's a little market up ahead with a gas station. The selection in the store isn't the best, but the bathroom is clean. Yeah, I'm just kidding. I'm pretty sure I've stopped at this exit not too long ago. Here we are. You can hit the head when I get back. The place looks empty, but you've got to watch out for grifters. We don't need any looky-loo's peeking in our trunk while we're gone. Here comes the attendant now. Tell him to fill her up with unleaded. Stay put while I go inside.

Okay, I'm ready to roll when you are. The cashier gave me a weird look when he rang me up, but I get that from just about everybody these days. I got you a bag of chips and some cupcakes. I picked up all the local newspapers, too. If you know what to look for, they're one of the best sources of information for this line of work.

The last time I was out this way, I was headed down the same road to Mount Vernon, Ohio. I had a lead on a bloodsucker in the area. You know this story, but it'll be good for you to hear it from the beginning, from my point of view. It's not like we don't have time to kill.

After the pit stop at the same station we just passed through, I headed on my way and as I got closer to Mount Vernon, I needed to find somewhere to set up shop. Before long, I came upon a sign for a place called the Evergreen Motel. Figuring this place was as good as any, I followed the next exit. As far as motels are concerned, I've seen them all, and the Evergreen was the same as the rest. The layout of the rooms formed a U-shape with two levels. An exposed metal staircase on each end led to the 2nd floor with a pool in the center of the U. After checking in with the clerk and renting a room for the night, I sat at the desk in my room to do some research. The room was dark, illuminated only by a small light built into the wall above. I dropped my stack of newspapers on the desk and started flipping through them. *The Columbus Dispatch, The News-Herald,* and *The Star-Beacon.* As you might have noticed, I pick up the paper anytime I have a chance. I'm always looking for the next job or for leads on the current one. Scanning for recent murders, disappearances, mutilations, hell... even high-profile individuals with a sudden change of disposition could be a lead worth following.

The front page of The News-Herald had an article about the space race. The Soviets just launched some new satellite with a cute name. Inside, the paper contained mostly world news, nothing local, which meant nothing pertinent to the case. I had little luck with the Columbus Dispatch as well, but there was an article in The Star-Beacon that caught my eye. The article detailed a string of local animal attacks in recent months. The victims' bodies were found mutilated and partially eaten. Most of the corpses had been dragged into the woods near a residential neighborhood. Local authorities chalked it up to a family of bobcats and were working with animal control to locate them. Town officials advised residents to stay out of the woods on the eastern edge of town, the area where they recovered the bodies.

Based on the article, it was hard to tell if the cops were using the bobcats as a cover story, or if they were as clueless as an elephant in the ocean. My guess was they were way over their heads because staying out of the woods wouldn't protect people from a vampire.

If they're desperate enough, those bastards will come right into your house while you sleep. My first order of business in the morning was to head down to the local police station and see if I could squeeze any more info out of them. For now, after countless hours on the road, I was ready for some shut-eye.

The next morning, after my first shower of the week. I rifled through my outfits and fished out a forest green blazer with matching pants and a beige stetson. After getting dressed, I headed down to the local sheriff's office with my Forest Ranger credentials and briefcase. I always keep an array of fake IDs, credentials or other documents that might come in handy when dealing with local authorities or convincing civilians I'm trustworthy. Don't judge me. I do what I have to do to get the job done.

Upon entering the small one story building, a lanky young man wearing a deputy's uniform, sitting behind a desk covered with stacks of papers, looked up from his work. "Howdy, what can I do you for? The name's Deputy Rick Morgan," he said with a wide grin. No offense, but I felt like smacking it off of him. I guess that's just me being old and grumpy.

I put on my best friendly face anyway and began, "Hi, my name is Wayne Westwood and I'm from the State Parks Department. I'm here about the recent animal attacks you've had. Nasty stuff. I've been looking into similar attacks throughout the region and wanted to confirm if this is the same predator I've been tracking."

"Oh sure, hold on a minute, mister," he replied, and turned his head to yell, "FRANK!!!"

Within a moment, an older gentleman with a red face and an enormous belly popped out from an office in the back of the room with an annoyed look on his face. "Rick, how many times have I told you not to yell like that? You almost gave me a goddamn coronary."

"Sorry boss, this guy's here from the Parks Department about those animal attacks we've had recently. I figured you'd want to know."

Waving me over, the big man put out his hand and introduced himself as Sheriff Frank Dailey. "Come on into my office... what did you say your name was?" and then, without waiting for a reply, continued, "Hell of a thing, these attacks. Townsfolk are on edge. No one will let their kids out. Our local animal control said they've never seen nothin' like it. I didn't know what to tell everyone, so we said it was a pack of bobcats, but I'm not so sure. I think it's gotta be something bigger, like a grizzly bear, but we don't normally get those in this area."

After we finished our introductions, I took a seat and Sheriff Dailey removed a manila folder from the top drawer on his desk. "Before I show you this, I gotta warn you, these pictures are not for the faint of heart," he said.

"Don't worry about me. Ten years on the job. Between hunting accidents and animal attacks, I've seen my fair share."

"Ok, but don't say I didn't warn you," the sheriff replied, as he spread out the contents of the folder, pushing it across the desk.

It was worse than I had been expecting. The first two victims were unrecognizable. The sheriff explained some of the corpses couldn't even be ID'd for several days. Photos from the first crime scene showed a man ripped in half. They found his lower extremities ten feet away from the upper half of his body. Deep gashes marked his abdomen and thigh, where the beast sunk its claws and teeth into his flesh before ripping the victim in two.

The second victim was found after a brief search when a beagle came back to its owner chewing on a metacarpal. The photos in the second case showed various appendages piled haphazardly on top of each other. Most of the flesh had been stripped from the bone and the coroner had to use dental records to identify the victim.

The most recent fatality was relatively lucky. Her face was still intact, but that didn't mean she would have an open casket funeral. A young woman in her thirties with dirty blond hair. She was known to the officers as a local prostitute and still recognizable, even with a large section missing from her throat. Only a few stringy tendons kept the victim's head attached to the rest of her body. It was clear from all three victims that their assailant had partially eaten the remains. That fact, along with the claw marks and the sheer strength required to perform these killings, led the police to label them as animal attacks.

While examining the crime scene photos, I noticed the sheriff kept his eyes averted from the gruesome pictures. When I finished looking them over he said, "I tried to tell ya, I ain't never seen nothin' like it, I can barely look at them. If you're plannin' on going out there, I can gather up a few deputies to help."

I knew right away that if he couldn't stomach looking at the pictures, he couldn't handle the action, and

I doubted the gawky deputy I met on the way in could either. "Thanks for the offer. I'm going to run down a few more leads and I'll let you know," I replied, not wanting to outright refuse the help and raise any suspicion. Lately, I came to prefer hunting alone, anyway. The locals had no clue what they were up against, and their weapons would barely slow the vampires down. More often than not, cops would just get in the way or end up dead. On the off-chance they survived the ordeal, I would be on the hook to explain what they just witnessed. I don't have the patience for babysitting. Once someone's had their eyes opened to the supernatural, that shit seems to follow them around, or maybe they're just more likely to notice what's already right in front of them. Either way, it becomes part of their life and I don't want to be responsible for that. It's why I prefer to ride solo. The job's easier that way. Each attachment is just another weakness. If you don't have anyone to care about, you won't have anyone to lose. At least, that's been my motto ever since my brother died.

Besides, I'd already seen enough to know what I was up against; a single, newly turned vampire. Only a new vampire on their own would tear a body to shreds like that and be so careless as to leave it virtually in plain sight. An experienced killer would know how to hide his tracks and not be so sloppy about the kill. I could handle a baby vamp on my own, or so I thought. After refusing help a second time on my way out the door, I headed to check out the area where the killings had taken place.

On my drive around town, I realized the extent of my exhaustion. Not just from a lack of solid sleep, although that was definitely part of it. I'm getting too old for this shit, but I know there is only one way out of this profession and it doesn't end with a dinner party and cake. The sooner you come to terms with that fact, the better off you'll be. There's a job that needs doing, and not as many hunters around to do it these days. The job is more important than being tired. It's more important than anything. Dad taught me that. Eventually, as you get older, your reflexes aren't what they used to be. Every hunter knows it's a dangerous game, and one of these days, those blood suckers will catch up with you. At that point, it's better to just pray for a quick end. There are no retirement homes for vampire hunters.

When you add all that to the fact that I've been hunting alone, my odds of long-term survival are about as good as a lobster at a clambake. It's been five months since I lost my brother, Rob. My best friend since we were in diapers. We did everything together, from playing football as kids to sharing our first beer in high school. Hell, we even shared a few ladies back in the day. It was only natural that we took up the family business when we came of age.

As kids, Dad was always on the road, working as a traveling salesman. At least, that's what we were told. Rob and I were smart kids. Dad was a tough guy, not some smooth talker. We never believed the traveling salesman bit. While he was gone, we used to make up all sorts of fantasies about him. The most common daydreams were some variation of him off working for the CIA on a top secret mission in Russia or Germany. Although Dad wasn't employed by any government agency, we were closer to the truth than we realized.

One day, when I was twelve and Rob was fourteen, Dad took us to his shed and told us it was time for 'the talk'.

At first, thinking of a different awkward conversation, Rob tried to brush it off, telling him we already knew about the birds and the bees. My father stopped him there and told us he had something much more serious to talk about. It was time we learned about the true McGrath family profession. The sacred duty in our family, passed down from generation to generation. Now that we were both old enough to know the truth, even if Ma didn't think so, they couldn't risk waiting any longer. From there, he explained to us about the creatures lurking in the night and by the next day, we were mighty eager to begin training for our new jobs as assistant vampire hunters. Over the next few years, he taught us everything he knew about vampires. Most importantly, how to track them and how to kill them. I aim to pass that knowledge on to you.

Although it's been over five months since my brother's passing, the memories play back like it was yesterday. We were following a lead just outside St. Louis, and after a week of late night stakeouts, we finally got a break. Watching some local college kids stumbling home from a bar, they were completely unaware of the vampire stalking them. Rob and I noticed the telltale signs immediately. For one thing, it was quiet. Completely quiet except for the murmurs and laughs of the inebriated kids. Even the crickets stopped chirping. Staying out of sight, we kept our eyes trained on the shadows, scanning for any movement.

We knew we weren't dealing with just a single vampire here, but a decent sized nest. The rash of missing person reports in a short time that led us to the area in the first place was proof of that. One vampire wouldn't need to feed more than twice a week, and if they kept someone alive in their lair... well, the vampire could last as long as the human could. The lack of bodies made that a strong possibility.

This is where the hard part came in. We needed the vampire to lead us back to its lair to make sure we found and eradicated all of them in one fell swoop. Plus, the missing persons' cases complicated things. There could be people alive being held inside the vampire's den. Sure, I don't mind playing the hero and saving any helpless bystanders, but eliminating the vampires is always the primary concern. If one escaped, it could alert the others to a hunter in the area. Once they got a whiff of danger, the rest would flee, and it could take years to find them again. All of this meant not interfering with what was about to happen.

We spotted the vampire crouching along an alley and when the couple happened by it, it stood, slowly approaching them. The man raised his hands in a shrug. He seemed to apologize, as if rejecting a beggar. The vampire continued to approach and tilted its head back, revealing its gaunt features. The beast opened its mouth, exposing the sharp fangs within. Before the man could react, the beast had its jaw clenched around his neck and the woman let out a cry. Releasing the man, who slumped to the ground, the vampire turned to the woman before she could escape or draw any more attention to them. Tears streamed down her cheeks as she backed away from the scene in front of her. Her eyes were fixed on her male companion, who lay motionless in the street. The vampire grabbed hold of her before she regained her wits and returned to finish his dying meal.

Rob and I watched the scene play out while hiding out of sight. I never claimed to be a saint, and it pained me to let those innocent people meet their demise, but it was the surest way to find the nest. After the monster finished its feeding, it headed off with the woman in tow. The vampire moved quickly, and we almost lost the trail, but the woman slowed it down enough for us to keep up.

Apparently the fact that we were tailing the creature hadn't gone unnoticed, and as we turned the corner to enter an alley between two large buildings, something dropped from the top of one of the structures, landing right on top of Rob. It clenched its mouth around his shoulder, shaking its head like a dog with a bone, tearing chunks of meat from Rob's neck. Blood sprayed in the air as Rob fell to the ground like a discarded trash bag. I called for him but it was already too late. Still in a state of shock, terror and rage burned inside me, but at that point, I noticed the other vampire had turned his attention on me.

I withdrew my Colt and fired, knocking the vampire back as he fell to one knee. The vampire smiled and rose to his feet, but the bullet hole in its chest fizzed, making a hissing sound. The vampire looked down at the wound in confusion. Regular ammunition won't stop these creatures, but I came prepared. I forged these bullets with holy water blessed by a bishop. Even though the small amount of holy water in the bullet won't kill the vampire, it will cripple the monster severely while its body works to purge the water from its system.

I turned to face the beast that killed my brother, who was now hunched over, drinking the blood that flowed freely from Rob's neck. I aimed at the creature, and it looked up just in time to see the gun go off. A split second later, the bullet entered its forehead, knocking the beast on its back with its legs kicking out involuntarily against the ground. I withdrew my machete and, with a few hefty swipes, removed the heads of both vampires as they lay on the ground in agony. After I completed the gruesome task, I kneeled by my brother's body to say a prayer. Still in a state of shock, I barely remember this part. Maybe I subconsciously tried to forget. I knew the likelihood of this day coming, but my emotions swirled with sadness and anger. I wanted to go home and forget all about these godforsaken creatures, but I had to continue on in search of the lair. I'd be back later to finish disposing of the bodies. At that point, I was on autopilot, letting my mind turn off and allowing instinct to control my body. There was only one other vampire to be dispatched. Unaware of the commotion outside, I snuck in and took it out swiftly. I burned the bodies of all three and collected my brother's remains before slipping off into the night to avoid answering questions when the cops showed up.

Oh yeah, I almost forgot. Two of the missing locals were being held by those bastards. I set the two girls free. They were barely alive, but saving those girls went a long way in helping ease my conscience about the couple we used as bait. I mean, nothing could make up for the ultimate sacrifice my brother made, but at least there was a small silver lining. I suggested to the girls that they leave any hints of the supernatural out of their stories to the police, lest they end up in a mental ward. The police would be more likely to believe in human trafficking or sexual deviants than the truth of the ordeal. Keeping it simple would hasten their return to their families and attract less scrutiny all around. They were in such shock, who knows what they would even remember or believe happened. Any word of vampires or the supernatural, and it's usually attributed to trauma. Then the victims end up spending the rest of their lives in the loony bin. Let's hope for their own sake the girls heeded my advice.

Anyway, sorry for the tangent, but it's something I thought you should know about me and about what this life is like, what it could cost you. If there is anyone that you care about, I suggest you forget all about them. For their sake as well as yours.

Where was I? Right. In your old stomping grounds of Mount Vernon, Ohio. There were still a few hours before sundown, but the long night ahead required plenty of preparation. I had just enough time for a quick nap to keep refreshed for the night. I stopped at the motel to recharge, ready my weapons, and pick up my belongings. There's always a chance I'll need to high-tail it out of there after a confrontation and before the locals pick up the pieces. I don't like answering questions, so it's best to be packed and ready to hit the road.

I researched the areas near town and found two spots the vampires might use for a hunting ground. There was a homeless encampment on the eastern end of town, and about a mile from that is a strip of seedy bars. It's an area where prostitutes frequently sell their wares.

Although I'd love to watch the ladies do their thing all night, I knew staking out the hookers could bring some unwanted attention down upon myself, so I figured setting up outside the homeless encampment would be the wiser choice. It was also a more secluded area, so the vampire might prefer a straightforward snatch and grab with fewer prying eyes.

The homeless encampment spread throughout an old abandoned farm. Some residents lived inside barns or sheds that were still standing in various states of disrepair. Rusted out cars and tractors littered the area with bicycles and other junk between. The rest of the people here lived in makeshift tents that were scattered among the fields. I attempted to speak with one of the inhabitants, a man with a scraggly beard, graying from age, but he gave off an unwelcoming vibe and an even worse smell, so I hung back to see how things played out.

I took up a position about fifty yards from my car under a tree. Close enough that I could get to it in a hurry but not a sitting duck in the driver's seat and easily spotted. This location gave me a clear vantage point of the main entry to the encampment while remaining under cover. This was the worst part. Sitting alone at night, waiting. At least during the long road trips, I've got my tunes to keep me company. And I don't have to worry about making too much noise or my legs cramping from being stuck in an awkward hiding spot. The bitch of the thing is, I could be sitting here in silence all night waiting for something that never happens. At least that night, I was well rested. The nap went a long way in helping me get through the night without having to fight dozing off every few minutes. When I'm laying in wait, I try not to let my mind wander too far. You have to stay alert, listening to every twig snap or leaf rustle for an approaching vampire while filtering out the white noise. The last thing you want is for one of these bloodsuckers to get the jump on you.

Patience paid off for me that night, because about fifteen minutes before midnight, I saw my target creeping towards a barn on the edge of the camp. I didn't need a closer inspection. I've seen enough fangs in my life, I can spot them a mile away. The way they carry themselves, especially when hunting, is a dead giveaway. The vampire's movements were both menacing and graceful like a fox as it slunk among the vegetation, inching closer to the barn.

I advanced on the vampire's position with my gun drawn. When the distance between us narrowed enough, I aimed and squeezed the trigger. The bullet exploded out of the barrel and buzzed towards the target, but almost as if in slow motion, the vampire turned its head towards me and smiled before it leaped out of the way at the last instant. I hate how fast those fuckers move. No creature should be able to move like that. It's not natural.

The thought barely had time to cross my mind before the monster knocked me over and had me pinned to the ground. I felt the vampire's claws digging into the flesh of my chest. I pushed back against the bastard with everything I had, but it was no use against its superhuman strength. The beast reared its head back, barring the long fangs that emerged from its mouth. At that point, I sighed and resigned to make peace with my fate when another blast rang out that sent the vampire staggering back off me.

It only took a moment for the monster to shake off the blast. The vampire rose to its full height with a look of rage on its face. I guess it didn't like being caught off-guard. I didn't know where the gunshot came from, but I'm not one to waste a second chance; and that moment was all I needed. I fired my gun at the monster, while its attention was diverted to the new assailant. The holy water bullet struck it right in the side of his head. A perfect shot, but still not lethal. I moved on the fallen vampire to finish it off, and what do you know? I looked up to see the scrawny deputy from the station in a state of shock, still pointing his shotgun at the vampire.

"Wow! What the heck was that thing!?" Deputy Morgan managed to say as he regained his senses. I ignored the question, returning my attention to the vampire. I had less than a minute to finish the job and think of an explanation. But the deputy had already seen too much, and I didn't have time to delay. I removed the head and lit the body on fire, performing the task with a swiftness that comes from years of practice and a healthy dose of fear. The easiest explanation for the deputy, of course, was the truth and the kid deserved that much for showing up when he did and saving my ass. I'd have to give the talk after all, but it beats the alternative.

So began the laborious process of explaining the truth behind what had been killing people in town. Hollywood's portrayal of vampires made the job easier. People are already familiar with them. It was just a matter of separating the fact from the fiction. It turned out Sheriff Dailey had told the deputy to tail me. Apparently, I didn't play my part well enough because they knew something was fishy about my story, but also knew they needed any help they could get.

I agreed to follow Rick to the station to back up his explanation to the Sheriff. Deputy Morgan and I were on a first name basis by then. Rick promised Sheriff Dailey wouldn't arrest me no matter how incredulous the story we told, and he was right. Although the sheriff asked me to be available for some followup questions, that is not something I usually oblige. Normally, I would have high-tailed it out of there, but something told me to stick around.

I needed some time to clear my mind from my near death experience, and I had a hunch you'd be calling me. I stayed the night at the motel to recuperate and got your call the next day. Now here we are, riding off into the sunset together like a pair of newlyweds. It takes a special kind of person to leave everything behind for this life, Rick. I know I might not sound like it, but I'm happy to have you as my apprentice and to pass the torch when the time comes. The world needs more hunters. I have a hunch the odds are stacked against us.

Born Again

S an Antonio, Texas
1993

William was in the middle of the strangest dream, but as he jolted awake, he couldn't remember any of the details. He only knew he wanted to find his way back to the fantasy as quickly as possible, but an odd sensation tickled his skin, preventing his return to slumber. He heard a mechanical sound in his ear. Water was hitting his face. *Where was he? Outside in the rain?* A pounding inside his skull made him bring his hand to his temple, and he began the strenuous task of opening his eyes.

He waited a moment for his vision to adjust and as his sight cleared, William found himself lying on the ground against a rock. The water, still hitting his face and in the process of soaking his clothes, was coming from a nearby sprinkler. He pushed himself up to his hands and knees, tried to stand, but his leg wobbled. Unable to support his weight, William stumbled, falling back to the ground. His face landed in the grassy mud he had been lying in. His legs felt numb from his odd sleeping position, as pins and needles pricked all along his lower extremities. Stretching them out to regain some circulation, he slowly stood again, this time using the rock as support. Glancing down at the stone, he noticed a carving in the rock. Some letters or an inscription. The stone he had slept against and that currently supported his shaky legs was a tombstone. He looked around and found himself in the middle of a cemetery. William knew the spot, not too far from his house, but had no recollection of coming here. It's not like he made a habit of hanging out in the graveyard.

His hands went back to his head, rubbing his temple and eye sockets in an attempt to dull the throbbing ache. *Think. How did I get here? Why would I pass out in the cemetery?* The answer came immediately. The only obvious reason, booze. Trying to remember the events of the previous night, it slowly came back to him. He remembered going out with his friend Josh who borrowed his older brother's ID. They went to a bar downtown but only drank a couple of beers, not usually enough to cause a blackout. Being seventeen years old, William didn't have the highest tolerance, but he had enough drunken nights to know he could handle more than that.

The sun seemed brighter than normal. The rays beating down from the sky above made sweat accumulate around his forehead, but William didn't notice the heat. In fact, his body felt cool considering the weather. Regardless of the temperature, the brightness of the sun caused his headache to overpower his thoughts, and he gave up any further attempts to piece together the events of the previous night. This was going to be a wicked hangover, and William wished he was home, under his covers, in bed. He squinted his eyes as he stumbled towards the cemetery's entrance, not looking forward to the walk home.

The walk to his house felt like the longest fifteen minutes of William's life. Each car that passed rumbled by like an earthquake, shaking the street. A horn blasted as he stumbled off the sidewalk onto the road. William flipped the motorist off as it passed by in a cloud of dust.

Something moved inside William's pocket, causing him to jump in surprise. The buzzing continued until he removed the object creating the commotion. His beeper. He had five messages from Josh. His friend tagged the latest one 911, meaning the matter was urgent.

William needed to get home and sleep off the rest of this hangover, then call his friend to fill in some of the previous night's blanks. As he stumbled to the front door, he prayed his parents weren't in the living room awaiting his entrance. God only knows how long they would give him the fifth degree until they finally allowed him to retreat to his quarters.

The front door was unlocked, as expected. William turned the handle and stepped through as quietly as possible so as not to arouse any unwanted attention. Luckily, his parents were nowhere in sight, so he made a direct route upstairs to his room. Upon arriving, he collapsed on his bed, not even bothering to get under his *Teenage Mutant Ninja Turtles* sheets. Within seconds, William was dead to the world, shivering despite the Texas heat. By then, he had forgotten about his dream from the cemetery, but upon his first moment of sleep, he picked up right where he left off.

This time, when William returned to his dream, an ominous feeling came over him. He could feel a dark presence all around him creeping closer. It was almost as if Death himself traveled alongside him. He pictured riding next to the horseman, not fearful of the harbinger but empowered by him. William felt the sensation of cold air as it smacked against his face. The icy breeze chilled his bones. He couldn't tell if he was falling or flying. Maybe he was floating. He looked ahead, but everything was cloudy. William tried to focus, but everything remained hazy, like he was wearing someone else's prescription glasses. With his vision blurred, his other senses heightened. He sniffed the air and immediately had the taste of raw meat in his mouth. The metallic taste of blood tickled his throat.

Unable to control his movements, William continued to hover along, following the trail of scents in the air and taking in his surroundings as he went. He noticed a person standing below him, who seemed unaware of William's presence. He continued floating, keeping pace with the person as he walked. William noticed something familiar about the young man but couldn't place it. As he floated closer, he realized he was looking down upon himself. Overwhelmed with strange sensations, he's never had a dream quite like this before.

bang-bang-bang

"William! When did you get home? You tracked mud all throughout the house! You know we take our shoes off inside the house. Your mother is going to have a fit when she sees this mess she'll have to clean. Helloooooo, anybody alive in there?"

Unexpectedly ripped out of his dream by his father's calls, his headache hadn't yet subsided and might have even felt worse due to sleep inertia. A shiver crawled through his body, making him feel like a giant millipede wiggled where his spine should be. William rolled over and put the pillow on his head to block the noise.
His dad's incessant pounding on the door didn't stop. Taming the rage that built inside of him, he replied in as calm a voice as he could muster, "Sorry Dad, I'm not feeling well. I'll clean it up later."

A huff on the other side of the door and he heard footsteps trudging away down the hall. William closed his eyes and eagerly crept back into his lucid dream. Again, he picked up right where he left off, still floating along as if on an astral plane. The people below, he now noticed many of them, seemed so happy. They frolicked along, enjoying nature and their surroundings, as if on a stroll through the forest. He saw children playing by a stream while the parents talked and laughed in the field, enjoying the summer breeze.

Even with the joy radiating from the scene below, something felt off. It looked as if everything was in technicolor but the hues became scrambled along the way, like the entire world had been put through a black light. William glanced above him for the first time. Ribbons of blue and red light streaked the sky and twisted in the air like party streamers, leading to a magnificent sun. The sun rained a purple hue across the land, but instead of warmth, the sun's rays brought icy cold with its reach, freezing everything in its path.

Even with this approaching ice storm, the people below, himself included, carried on without a care in the world. William tried to call to them, to warn them, but his jaw became stuck in a silent scream as the sun's rays reached him. The freeze extended through his body. Even his eyes remained glued in place, gazing at the stars that speckled the sky and illuminated the heavens as the sun rained destruction below.

Again, William awoke. This time of his own accord. Just like in his dream, his whole body stung with cold. He hadn't a clue what time it was or how long he had been sleeping. Nausea crept through his intestines up to his stomach. Feeling about to retch, he tripped out of bed to the door and stumbled into the hallway, making a clamor as he went. By the time he reached the hall, his nausea had turned to thirst. He needed to get some water. He staggered into the kitchen as fast as his legs would go while still maintaining his balance. William grabbed a water jug from the refrigerator and put it directly to his lips, pouring the clear liquid into his mouth. No sooner did it touch his tongue than he spat it back out again, shocked by the cold temperature, which only added to the constant shivers that visibly shook his body. He dropped the plastic jug, letting it fall to the floor, making a gurgling sound as it spilled its contents onto the white tile.

William's mouth was so dry, but he needed warmth. He turned on the faucet with the dial turned to hot, waiting impatiently for the temperature to rise. When it did, he submerged his mouth into the scalding stream. Soothed by the heat that seared his skin, he swallowed gulp after gulp, letting the warmth fill his belly. The heat gave William the feeling of sitting by a campfire on a chilly evening, but the water did nothing to quench his growing thirst. He felt his tongue cracking and his stomach turning. Pain shot through his kidneys. "What happened to me last night?" he said, unintelligible to anyone but himself.

He searched his mind, still hazy of the previous night's events. He tried to remember what could have led to his current state. This was like no hangover he'd ever felt before. At the bar with his friend Josh, someone must have slipped something into his drink or drugged him. It was the only explanation. William remembered the string of messages from his pager. Maybe his friend would have some insight for him. He picked the phone off the cradle on the wall and dialed Josh's number.

As soon as his friend answered, William said, "Hey Josh, what the fuck happened last night?"

"Yo, my man! I've been paging you, but didn't want to be a bother in case you were still getting lucky. You don't remember? The chick from the bar last night? Didn't you go home with her? She had her eye on you all night and then she came in for the kill, so to speak. I won't say I wasn't jealous, but I'm no cock block. She was stunning, and you hit it off with her right away. You told me not to wait up, so I headed home while you were still partying it up. What happened? Is everything ok?"

"Yeah... yeah. I just seemed to have blacked out and got a killer hangover. I'm fine. I'll talk to you later."

William hung up the phone, just as confused as before the call. Something didn't add up. If this girl looked half as good as his friend said, she wouldn't need roofies to convince him to go home with her. There must be another explanation for his missing memories.

Still lost in his thoughts, the kitchen lights turned on, causing William to throw his hands up in defense of the blinding light. The water in his stomach suddenly felt like a foreign substance that needed to be expelled. His father stood in the entryway to the hall, blocking William's egress. William had half a mind to plow right through his father and make his way to the bathroom.

"What's going on, Will? You don't look well at all, are you ok?" his father asked upon seeing his son feebly standing before him. His father's gaze moved towards the mess on the floor. Almost the entire gallon of water had spilled onto the tile.

William attempted to reply, but pain shot through his jaw with the slightest movement of his mouth. The only sound that escaped his throat was a pitiful croak.

Concerned for his son's unwillingness or inability to muster a response, and not wanting to see him in such a state, he kept his eyes glued to the floor and said, "You better go lie down. Your mother is going to have a fit about this mess." Glancing up quickly, he added, "Is that blood on your shirt? That won't come out, you know."

William looked at his clothes and noticed the dried blood that stained his once white shirt. The mixture of splattered mud from his slumber in the cemetery along with the mysterious blood guaranteed this shirt was ruined. Any care for the soiled clothing quickly faded as pain continued to shoot through his head. The thumping repeated in rhythm, followed by the flowing sound of liquid. Unable to suppress his insides any more, he shoved past his dad to the bathroom and barely made it inside before throwing up. He could feel the muscles in his stomach clenching to expel the hot water from his gullet. The room immediately filled with a sour stench, reeking from the bile clinging to the sink.

William looked at himself in the mirror. For everything that he was feeling, he didn't look half bad. His face remained pale from the hangover, but all of his blemishes were gone. His normally pimple ridden skin seemed soft and smooth. If only the throbbing pain in his head would go away. He closed his fist and punched it against his skull, causing instant regret as the pain only intensified. The ache caused his whole body to shiver. William looked himself in the eyes, which had clouded over, blurring his vision. The harder he stared, the cloudier everything became. He barely recognized himself. He searched his mind for answers and slowly slipped back into a trance-like state, letting his mind wander.

He was back in the neon fields, the blue sun shooting icicles from above, but this time he walked among the others in his own body. Everyone seemed so carefree, paying no mind to the dangers above. They gathered at the river that flowed through the clearing, kneeling to drink from the running water. William recognized the girl. The one from the bar. His memories cleared as he drew close to her, and his clouded vision came into focus.

Dancing in the club, she had intoxicated him. He took a deep breath and smelled the pheromones radiating from her. The scent was like nothing he has smelled before. He wanted to devour her. They swayed to the music, pressing their bodies against each other. Her tongue danced in his mouth and darted away just as quickly, leaving him in a constant state of wanting more. How long this went on for, he couldn't say, but eventually they exited the club and walked down the street together, holding hands, touching. His mind was fixated on her and then... kissing, teeth, blood, sex, darkness.

Still inside his dream, the same girl motioned for him to join her at the river. William sensed danger and tried to stop himself, but he advanced against his will as if he was a passenger in his own body. The water dripped down her slender arms as she scooped it into her mouth. The liquid dribbled from her mouth, staining the front of her shirt. *Strange. Water is clear, why was it turning her shirt red?* The fluid that spilled from between her lips was blood. With that thought, the river surged next to them, sloshing blood on the banks and spraying his feet.

William's mouth salivated at the sweet smell from the river of blood flowing at their feet. He kneeled next to the stream and against every fiber of his will, he cupped his hands, filling them with the crimson fluid and brought his hands to his mouth, finally quenching the thirst that had been building inside of him all day. William closed his eyes and released himself to the taste and pleasure within.

"WHAT THE FUCK!"

William was dragged back out of his dream again. Who keeps interrupting him? At the best part too. He could almost taste the blood from his dream in his mouth. William tried to make sense of his surroundings and what the commotion was about. It was a woman's voice this time, his mother.

"This has gone too far. I don't know how to deal with this." His mother said. Her voice wavered as she spoke in shock and disgust. She stood in the hall with the door to the bathroom open, looking in at her son. William was on his knees, hunched over the trash can. From his mouth dangled a small white string as he sucked the last of the dried blood from a discarded tampon he picked out of the garbage.

He came out of the daze and finally saw what his mother had been screaming about. The embarrassment of being caught in this strange act by his mom crept through him, but the urge to finish his snack outweighed any other cares, so he turned from her and focused back on the task at hand. To William's chagrin, the cotton in his mouth had lost its flavor, but he now had a taste of the fluid he craved. He spat the tampon on the floor and sniffed the air. His attention returned to his mother, who hadn't stopped yelling, even though William had tuned out her words. He smelled the blood gathering in his mother's panties, where another delicious cotton popsicle lay.

The pounding returned, but this time it wasn't from the pain inside his head. That ache still lived within him, but this beating came from the hallway where his mother stood. The sound of her pulse pumping blood through her veins. He heard each beat, followed by a whoosh as the liquid circulated throughout her body. The same blood that flowed through the river in his dream. The same blood he sampled from the garbage.

"Are you even listening to me?" his mom continued. "I think you are past the age for a sex talk, but it might be a good idea for you to speak to a professional. I'm sure your father can find someone for you to talk with about your... whatever this is."

The pain returned to William's head now, but instead of the dull throb emanating at the top of his skull, these sharp jolts shot down the front of his face, causing him to recoil in agony. If he didn't know better, he thought his skull might fracture, exploding chunks of bone everywhere. Instinctively, he started digging his fingers in his mouth to ease the pressure, scraping at the gums. His teeth pushed on each other, as if his mouth was too small to contain them. His upper jaw burned. He needed to snuff out the flames.

His mother stared at the spectacle before her. With her son's mouth open, she saw his teeth growing before her eyes and a wild, feral look came over him. She instinctively took a step back, but before she could take a second step, he was on her. He held her by the arms with his newly formed fangs submerged deep into her neck. Her carotid artery was hard at work, pumping blood from her neck into her son's mouth. With each spurt of blood he ingested, the hunger pains eased, replaced by a calm feeling. He continued drinking, tasting the succulent flavor. His first taste of congealed clots from the garbage seemed flavorful at the time but now he found true gratification. This fresh blood is what he craved.

William dug his jowls further into his mother's flesh, tearing away the muscle to get deeper into her shoulder, sucking as much moisture from her body as he could. He felt his mother's pulse come to a crawl. He pulled away instinctively as the life left her body. Having drank his first full meal, William's transformation was complete. He felt the strength surging through his body. Feeling like a million bucks, he bounded out the front door in search of a new life filled with adventure.

His father, who had watched the scene unfold, called after him, "Who is going to clean up this mess?"

Tourist Trap

B ran, Romania
  1983

"Hurry up! The town car is here and our flight leaves in 45 minutes!" Just as the words left David's mouth, Jessica turned the corner, lugging a large suitcase down the stairs. "Jeeze, how much stuff do you need for a week?" he added upon seeing her.

"This is the small one. I need you to grab the other bag from the bedroom," she replied.

With a grumble, David trekked up to get the other suitcase. He knew better than to argue.

"Where are the kids?" she asked as they passed on the stairs.

"Jeremy's already in the car. You know how excited about this trip he's been. It was his graduation present, after all. I'll check on Ashley."

After encouraging his daughter along and carrying one of her bags as well, they squeezed everything into the car and were off to the airport.

"I can't believe you picked Transylvania for our family vacation. You're so weird," Ashley said to her brother, rolling her eyes. "I'd rather be working on my tan in the Bahamas instead of freezing in some godforsaken mountain range with a name I can't even pronounce."

"It's actually Romania," David chimed in. After a blank stare from his daughter, he continued, "The country we're going to is Romania, and the Carpathian mountains are not hard to pronounce. You know your brother has always had a thing for horror movies. Besides, next year will be your choice... provided you pass your senior classes," he said with a chuckle.

The overnight flight allowed the Lund family to sleep during most of the eight hour trip to Munich, except for Jeremy, who stayed up to watch the in-flight movie. He would have preferred a horror movie like *The Evil Dead* or *Poltergeist,* but knew they needed to play something family friendly, so he didn't mind settling for *Superman II.* Jeremey planned to catch up on his rest during their five hour layover before connecting to Sibiu Airport in Romania but once arriving in Munich, he realized that might not be possible. After standing in customs and check-in lines for over two hours, they finally made it to their gate, with a couple of hours to spare. Enough time for a power nap, but the busy terminal and constant announcements only allowed him to doze off briefly. Ashley purchased some snacks and a magazine from the duty-free store. Jessica passed the time reading a smutty romance novel, regardless of how embarrassed her husband became around them.

Finally, David, who had been paying close attention to the boarding announcements, trying to translate as he listened, jolted the rest of the family from their seats. "This is ours!" he said, jumping to his feet. He grabbed two bags from the floor and ushered his family towards the gate.

Jeremy napped for another hour on the connecting flight, which gave him a small energy boost for his arrival at Bran Castle. He regretted staying up to watch Superman, but he'd have to make do.

Upon landing in Sibui airport, as promised, a gentleman holding a sign with their name, waited for them at the arrival gate. The portly man wore a dark gray vest that looked a size too small, a long overcoat with a wide lapel, and a medium-sized top hat.

David approached the man with the sign. "Hello, I think you must be our driver. I'm David Lund. This is my family."

"Good morning, Mr. Lund," the man replied in a deep voice with a thick accent, taking his time between words. "I hope you have pleasant trip. My name is Bogdan. If you be so kind to follow me to truck. Together, I drive you to castle."

On hearing the word truck, Jeremy said, "I thought this would be a carriage ride like in the movie. I saw one in the brochure."

Bogdan replied, "You see original carriage at the castle. I drive truck, Mercedes. We not use carriage in 50 years. These roads, very dangerous. Steep and many creatures in woods looking for meal. Anyway, it still long drive and many chance for nice view from truck."

David apologized for his son's attitude, but Bogdan brushed it off, noting that many guests ask about the carriage. Between the accent and monotonous tone of his voice, David couldn't tell if the man was joking or annoyed. Regardless, he planned on giving the driver a substantial tip upon arrival to ensure there was no ill will. The group departed the terminal following Bogdan's lead to a green Mercedes-Benz G Wagon.

They transversed many narrow roads that zig-zagged through a thick forest steeply up the mountain. After seeing the terrain, David was glad they had 4-wheel drive. Bogdan had been telling the truth about the views on the way up from the truck. Green vegetation covered the entirety of the lush mountains albeit for a few rocky crags scattered among the trees. Permanent snow capped the taller peaks in the distance. Dense forests covered most of the mountains with oak and beech trees, mixed with pines and many other varieties throughout.

Jessica enjoyed watching the trees pass by. Living in a city, she didn't get the chance to see such natural beauty as often as she'd like. She might have been paying closer attention to the scenery than Bogdan would have liked because, after a while, she noticed the same landmark going by again and again.

"Excuse me, are we going in circles? I've seen us pass this area before," she asked.

Bogdan replied, "Bran Castle only open gates in evening. No entrance during day. We must wait before arrive. Mountain hard to drive at night. I drive at day and arrive at dark."

The family understood this dog and pony show was part of the 'vampire castle' experience, but their stomachs growled with hunger and they were eager to arrive.

Finally, after navigating numerous hairpin turns, with Jessica and Ashley often feeling like the entire vehicle was about to tumble down the cliff, the road opened to a field of rolling hills. Situated on a sweeping hill was Bran Castle. The magnificent stone walls of the castle, peppered with windows throughout, led up to circular spires capped by rusty red-tiled roofs. The road followed a steep incline to a bridge supported by huge stone pillars.

The driver said, "The drawbridge is now permanently in down position, because entrance to castle is eight meters from ground. That is twenty six feet for you Americans. This prevent intruders in old days."

By the time the Mercedes reached the half-way point on the bridge, the large wooden gates began to open. The truck passed through them and entered a tiered courtyard with a stone floor laid out across multiple connecting levels. The Mercedes parked on the middle level of the courtyard between a set of stone stairs leading to the lower level and a rock wall separating an upper area. From inside the center courtyard, the sprawling castle looked like a maze of arches, passageways, and balconies. A covered walkway ran along the upper level. A large door in the corner of the courtyard opened and out stepped a slender man wearing a similar outfit to the driver. Although he was clearly older than Jeremey's parents, his age was hard to place. The man's wrinkled skin looked akin to someone in his nineties, but his brisk movement across the courtyard implied a man much younger than that.

"Good evening and welcome to Bran Castle, or as many know it... Castle Dracula. My name is Marius...

Tepes," said the man as he greeted the guests. Although his accent was thick and he talked with a waver in his voice, it was clear Marius spoke better English than the driver. "Please, follow me to your chambers to drop off your things. I can have the chef prepare some food... if you are hungry. When you are ready, I am available to give you a tour... of the castle."

To Jeremy's dismay, unlike the classic story, the caretaker was clearly not the same man who had driven them here. The group followed Marius into the castle, as he told the guests about the castle's rich history. Massive dark oak beams ran along the ceiling, contrasting the white plaster walls. The dark wood floor matched the exposed beams, giving the interior a gothic look. Although much care had been taken to preserve the original design aspects of the castle, the stewards of the castle made some updates and necessary additions over the centuries. The castle housed over 60 rooms; however, many were off-limits to the guests and used for storing antique furniture or other ancient treasures.

"Is this where you warn us not to venture off alone in the castle or we might get eaten by a vampire?" Ashley asked with a hint of sarcasm.

Marius smiled at her. "It may be wise to take your own advice."

Jessica noticed a sinister look in his eye, but brushed it aside. She replied, "I'm not worried about being eaten, but I could definitely see myself getting lost in these corridors."

On the way to their rooms, Marius pointed out an elegant lounge where they were welcome to spend time later. Jeremy's eyes went right to the fully stocked bar at the rear of the room. "Oh, we'll be coming here later for sure," he said, planning to take advantage of the lower drinking age in Europe.

After showing the guests to their rooms, Marius offered to have some food prepared in the dining room. They had two adjacent bedrooms, with the parents in one room and the children in another. Jeremy declined the offer of food, opting instead to catch up on some more rest so he could enjoy the night.

"Would you like me to bring you back something to eat after your nap?" Jessica offered.

"Sorry to interrupt, but food is only to be eaten... in the dining room," said Marius. "We wouldn't want to make a mess in the bedroom, would we?" Marius led David, Jessica and Ashley around a corner and down another long hall to a magnificent dining room.

Until this point, the rest of the castle's interior walls had been white and made of plaster, but in this room, ornate moldings had been carved into the wooden walls from floor to ceiling. Paintings of past owners or ancestors of the estate occupied the only open spots on the walls. On the table sat large platters of various sliced meats, cheeses, breads, and salads.

"Please help yourself I will return shortly to check on you," said Marius as he left the guests to enjoy their meal.

"This place seems a little creepy, don't you guys think?" asked Ashley. "Not your average all-inclusive resort."

"I think that's the point." said David. "Take a closer look at that portrait. Remind you of anyone?" he asked.

"It's a spitting image of Marius!" exclaimed Jessica. "And it's dated from the 1700s. How is that possible?"

"I'm sure it's just a prop. You know, to add to the creepy atmosphere," replied David. "You ladies will have a better time if you play along with the show."

After eating their fill, Marius returned and led the group back to their chambers. On the way, he said, "I can assure you, there are no... props in this castle. Everything here is... authentic. It is said my family has distinct features. I get mistaken for my father... often."

Jessica and Ashley gave each other a look, wondering how Marius heard their conversation from earlier. Back in the room, they found Jeremy awake, looking out the window. "Couldn't sleep. I'm ready to explore the castle. What's up next?" he asked as they entered.

Marius, still outside the door, offered a suggestion. "If you would like to follow me on a walk through the castle grounds, you can see more of our... beautiful estate. I must admit the gardens have become somewhat... overgrown in recent years, though they are still magnificent."

On their stroll through the grounds, Marius took notice of Jessica's interest in the landscaping. "I'm happy someone takes the time to appreciate... nature. The gardens are my favorite part... of the castle," he said, addressing Jessica. "Even if the guide book took away a half star for their current state. To me, they are just as magical as when they were built."

"They are quite charming," replied Jessica. "I wish I could have seen what they looked like back then." Taking in the scenery and imagining the castle's original state would end up being the highlight of Jessica's week. She didn't care much for her son's horror movies or creepy castles, but David had framed this to her as a peaceful vacation in the mountainous European countryside. That had been more than enough for her to sign off on the trip. She definitely planned on coming back to take her time and relax in the gardens again.

Jeremy, who seemed less interested in the flowers, had been admiring the architecture of the castle when he called out, "Hey do you see that?" He pointed to a window on the upper level. "Excuse me Marius, I thought you said we had the place to ourselves. I just saw someone in that window," he said.

Marius replied, "It is true, you are the only guests at the castle this week. But we do have family members who live here at the estate and they help.... how do you say... enhance the experience for our guests. Maybe you will run into them later... in the lounge."

David said, "Oh, that's fine. We don't expect you to cook and clean and do everything yourself."

"The lounge sounds nice. When can we head over there?" Jeremy asked.

Marius turned to Jeremy and replied, "Anytime you'd like, of course. We can head that way now if it pleases you."

In the lounge, a beautiful dark-haired woman sat alone against the bar. She held an old-fashioned cigarette holder. Her long white dressing gown draped to the floor, hiding the stool she was perched upon, giving her the effect of a floating ghost. She didn't seem to take any notice of the Lund family as they entered and sat on a velvet couch near the hearth. Jessica inquired to Marius about the fireplace, to which he responded it was no longer in use and was now just for decorative purposes.

Marius offered drinks to the group. Since Ashley was still seventeen, her mother made sure her drink was non-alcoholic. After pouring their requested libations, Marius left them to enjoy the rest of the evening. The cigarette smoke wafting from the bar annoyed Jessica, but as a guest in a foreign land, she knew she'd have to make do. Jeremy ached to try his luck at talking to the lady at the bar, but knew better than to attempt while his parents were in the room to embarrass him. His father saw the boy's stares at the young lady and sensed his nervousness. Luckily, David took the hint and, after finishing his drink, the adults excused themselves to their room, allowing the kids to stay a while longer.

Jeremy approached the bar, placing his glass down as he perused the selection for another drink. "What are you drinking?" he asked the mysterious woman.

She finally turned to look at him and with a smile replied, "I don't think you will like what I'm having, but I suggest you try our house special. It's a local plum brandy." She pointed to a bottle containing a golden liquid.

Now face to face, he noticed the paleness of her skin. Jeremy had seen his fair share of basement dwellers who didn't get any sun, but this woman didn't look like your average gaming nerd. At this thought, he remembered what Marius had said earlier in the gardens about the family helping enhance the experience. He suspected her to be an actor playing the part of a vampire, complete with a professional makeup job and all. His spirits dampened at the thought of the lady being paid to keep him company. He brushed the thought aside, wondering instead just how far she would go to make sure the guests had a memorable stay. Despite her heavy-handed makeup, she had an unnatural beauty about her. Even if he had to tip a few hundred dollars, it would be worth it to be with a woman like that.

Jeremy inspected the bottle she had suggested. He couldn't understand any of the words on the label, but he wasn't about to let that stop him from enjoying a glass. Jeremy had little experience with women and usually preferred to stay home and watch a slasher movie than try to pick up girls, but something about this one mesmerized him and shed his inhibitions.

"I am Elizabeth, Princess of the Castle. In case you were wondering," she said in an impassive tone. They raised their glasses in a toast. "To youth," she announced.

Jeremy followed suit. A real princess or not, he didn't care. His one track mind stayed fixed on how to get her back to his room. His hopes, however, quickly deflated when he noticed that, despite his advances, Elisabeth's attention was focused on his sister across the room.

"Sorry, but she's not interested in…" Jeremy stopped mid-sentence when he saw that Ashley had looked up and, to his surprise, had a sultry gaze in her eyes and smirk to match. She was staring back at Elisabeth and approached the bar. Elisabeth got up from her seat and took hold of Ashley's hand. She placed a gentle kiss on it.

Elisabeth turned to Jeremy and said, "Sorry, but I think she's more my sisters' type."

A stunned look came over Jeremy's face. He barely got the word out of his mouth as the princess led Ashley out of the room. "Sisters?" By the time he snapped out of his shock, he stepped out into the hallway after them, but the duo had disappeared without a trace.

Furious at his sister, he stormed back to his room. She had always been boy crazy and never showed the slightest attraction to women and now suddenly she does this, on his dream vacation no less. Still... something about Elisabeth was intoxicating. Part of him couldn't blame Ashley for succumbing to the princess's charm. Another part of him still thought she only did it to spite him for not choosing a beach vacation. He pondered the possibilities. *Yeah, right, he thought. She'll never go through with it.*

Elisabeth's lesbian adventure with his sister must have been the last thing on his mind before falling asleep because it filled his dreams that night. Not just the two of them, Elisabeth had two sisters in the fantasy as well. Normally, Jeremy would be repulsed by any sort of dream having to do with Ashley and sex but this dream was different. It felt so real his body tingled in his sleep. He awoke with a jolt, wiping his brow. Jeremy's shirt, soaked with sweat, clung to his body. His sheets were also damp enough from sweat, he took no notice of the mess he made in his pants. Breathing in and out deeply to calm down, he noticed Ashley sleeping soundly in her bed. *What time did she get back? What time is it now?* He didn't know.

Taking a quick shower and meeting up with his parents, Jeremy realized he too had slept later than planned and lunch would be served shortly. Ready to put the previous night behind him and shake off the weirdness of his dream, Jeremy took a seat and helped himself to a delicious meal of mici (spicy sausage) and stuffed cabbage.

After finishing, they returned to the room and found Ashley still sleeping. Having already slept through lunch, they decided to wake her lest she miss dinner as well. Normally a light sleeper, it was rather difficult for them to rouse her. David had to give her a good nudge before she finally opened her eyes. She sat up, letting the light hit her face. The group was taken aback at her pallid complexion. Her eyes fluttered, unable to stay open for more than a second.

"Honey, are you ok? You don't look well," David said to his daughter.

Jeremy replied for her, "She's fine, probably just a little hung over. Ash made a new friend last night and stayed up late."

David's expression flickered between anger and concern. He said, "Your brother might be old enough to have a few beers, but you are still underage, even here. I hope you learned your lesson about drinking too much. You'll have plenty of time to think about it when we get home, since you'll be grounded for the next month."

Ashley rocked back and forth, sitting up in bed in a daze, with her arms wrapped around her knees. She didn't hear a word her father said. David held his frustration back before it boiled over. He turned to go and added, "Whatever, let her miss dinner. That will teach her," and left the room.

Hangover or not, Jessica was filled with concern for her daughter. She helped Ashley back down and tucked her in with a kiss on the forehead. The kiss left a surprising tingle on Jessica's lips. She was not expecting her daughter's touch to be so cold. On their way to dinner, David charged Jeremy with making sure his sister stayed out of trouble for the rest of the trip. Jeremy, still jealous over how the previous night's events played out, happily agreed.

The rest of the family enjoyed another delicious dinner filled with course after course of meats and vegetables, many of which the guests couldn't even name. After dinner, they spent some time in the lounge again, where Marius offered David and Jeremy cigars.

David accepted. Jeremy declined but then said, "Unless it happens to be filled with the good stuff."

Marius looked offended at the implication, not understanding Jeremey's meaning. He replied, "Of course, we have only the finest... tobacco. These cigars are hand-rolled here in town."

Jessica looked at Jeremy sternly while David apologized again for his son. David enjoyed a fine glass of port with his cigar, when he noticed two dark-haired women enter the lounge. They spoke softly in what must have been Romanian while pouring themselves drinks at the bar. Laughing during pauses in their conversation, they shot mischievous glances at the family seated at the other end of the room. Jeremy became awestruck once again. He already knew Elisabeth, whom he'd met the night before. Strangely, Jeremy recognized the other woman from his dream. One of Elisabeth's sisters. She looked uncannily similar to Elisabeth, only a few years younger. Déjà vu overwhelmed Jeremy. He didn't understand how he could dream of someone he'd yet to meet. He was eager to talk to them and find out how late they kept Ashley out the previous night. David noticed Jeremy's constant glances at the women and sensed his anticipation. Regardless, he was still angry about these ladies getting his underage daughter drunk and decided to say something. As David approached, he could feel his courage deflating like an old balloon. Suddenly, he forgot what he was going to say.

Before he had a chance to open his mouth, Elisabeth said, "I promise, Mr. Lund, we didn't give your daughter any liquor last night. We had fun with her, might have kept her up a bit past her bedtime, but I can promise she was not drunk."

Elisabeth's sister swayed on her stool, playing with a toothpick in her mouth. David felt compelled to strike up a conversation with the ladies and before long, was laughing along with them. Feeling his wife's stares burning a hole through the back of his head, he reluctantly thanked the young ladies and bid them farewell.

"What the hell was that?" Jessica asked.

"I inquired about Ashley. Apparently, she didn't have anything to drink last night. She stayed up late with them. That's it."

"I know my daughter and that is not just staying up too late," Jessica barked in reply. "You'd probably believe anything those women told you."

"Pardon the intrusion, madam, but I can assure you, your daughter did not have any... alcohol last night," Marcus said, appearing out of nowhere. "If she is unwell, maybe she caught a sickness on her travels here. I would be happy to send someone... to attend to her."

"No, no, that won't be necessary," said David. "We were about to head back to our room ourselves. We can peek in on her. We will give you a shout if we need anything."

Now alone, Jeremy joined the ladies at the bar. He was eager to hear about last night's escapades with his sister. Immediately, he noticed the rosy pink blush on both of their cheeks and unnaturally bright red lips. Quite the change in Elisabeth's complexion from the night before. This raised his hopes that the women were done up for a night out. Jeremy figured with two females, his chances were doubled.

"You ladies are looking extra lovely tonight. Any big plans for the evening?" he asked, breaking the ice.

Elisabeth's sister smiled at him. "Ahh, so you must be Jeremy. I've heard much about you. We had an enchanting evening with your sister last night. My name is Ileana." she said, a sly smile creeping across her face.

"It's nice to meet you, Ileana. You look strangely familiar. Must be the family resemblance to your sister," he said, inching closer to the women. "So, what did you end up doing with my sister last night? She looked to be in rough shape today," he asked.

Ileana leaned over to whisper in Jeremy's ear, her cool breath making the hairs on his neck stand. A shiver surged through his spine. "As for last night, well, we don't kiss and tell. Maybe you'll get a taste tonight though," she said.

This was even better than Jeremy had been hoping for. Without putting in any effort, the younger sister was already flirting with him. She could be teasing, but by her mannerisms, he felt his chances were good. As for the possibility of being with two sisters at once, he could barely contain his excitement. Taking a breath, he slowed his thoughts. He didn't want to get ahead of himself. He would be more than content with either lady.

It turned out the women wasted no time in expressing their desires. Ileana had taken hold of Jeremy's hand and gently tugged him toward the hallway. Even Elisabeth seemed to be interested, motioning with her finger to follow. Upon realizing they were taking him back to his room, he stopped to ask if they could go somewhere else. He knew his sister was still sleeping inside.

The women ignored his plea. Jeremy remembered how hard it was to wake his sister earlier and figured they could get pretty far while she slept. If she woke in the middle of their threesome, so be it. Awkward, but not worth passing up this once in a lifetime opportunity. When they arrived at his room, he opened the door and was surprised to find that Ashley was not alone. He immediately recognized Maria, the third sister from his dream. He took in a deep breath at the sight of her and he felt the blood rush to his groin. His eyes went straight to her exposed chest. The milky white color of her breasts matched the rest of her naked body with large nipples only a shade pinker than her skin. She straddled Ashley in bed, who lay as clothesless as her companion. Their bodies undulated in rhythm. Hinting at Ashely's lesbian experience was one thing, but seeing his sister having sex with another female was something Jeremy would be happy to live his whole life without seeing. Nevermind that just a few hours ago she was sick as a dog. Jeremy's shocked gaze lingered for only a second before he turned to the ladies on his bed. Ileana and Elisabeth had already begun pulling at the laces of their shirts. He quickly decided the room was large enough. Ashley could easily be ignored.

The two sisters had him hypnotized. He crawled on the bed, grabbing hold of Ileana and pressing his lips firmly against hers, pushing his tongue into her mouth. She put her hands at Jeremy's sides and pulled his shirt over his head. Elisabeth had already unbuttoned his pants, exposing bright green boxer briefs that could barely contain his growing erection. Pulling his underwear down and taking hold of his manhood, she ran her tongue along the shaft. Ileana, not wanting to miss out on the fun, joined her sister between Jeremy's legs. He leaned back, putting his arms behind his head, barely able to believe his luck and hoping this wasn't another dream.

As he waited for the second woman to put him in her mouth as well, he felt immense pressure on his thigh, followed by a sharp pinch. He bolted upright, his gaze focused on the activity at his nether region. His eyes widened, and he choked on a gasp of air when he discovered Ileana biting down on his thigh. Blood streamed from the intersection of her lips and his leg. Even worse, Elisabeth exposed her own long razor-sharp teeth, and bit directly into his erect penis.

Stricken with panic, he attempted to push the women away, but his arms and legs were paralyzed. Sweat dripped into his eye, causing it to burn. Jeremy glanced over at the adjacent bed. Maria was still riding Ashley, but now blood covered Maria's mouth. The bright red liquid dripped off her chin, onto her bare chest. Blood squirted from a wound in Ashley's neck, but her face still had a look of utter pleasure. A feeling of nausea rose from Jeremy's stomach. He tried to come to terms with this reality. Everything spun around the room. The walls felt like they were closing in on him. His vision faded.

The next morning, David and Jessica sat in the dining room. Marius ensured that a full breakfast waited for them each morning when they woke. Today's meal included vegetable omelets, fresh fruit and coffee. "I wonder if Jeremy had a good time last night. I know he wanted to talk with those girls. They looked a little out of his league, but hopefully he didn't strike out completely. He could use some lessons with the ladies, but I guess I was just as awkward when I was his age. Full of courage, but could never close the deal."

"Oh, don't be silly. You closed the deal with me just fine," Jessica said with a giggle. Jeremy still has years to figure that stuff out. Plus, that's quite hypocritical. He's only one year older than Ashley. If those girls at the bar were guys, you would have never even left her alone with them."

David knew his wife was right, but he couldn't help rooting for his boy while still being overprotective of his little girl. "You got me," he replied. "I hope Ash is feeling better today, otherwise she'll miss the rest of our trip. We should check in on her. The car is scheduled to bring us back down the mountain later this evening. I can't imagine that ride with her being sick the whole way."

The couple peeked in on the kids when they finished eating. Although not wanting to wake Jeremy, their concern for Ashley outweighed any worries of waking their son. Jessica turned the doorknob slowly so as not to disturb the kids inside, but as the door creaked on its hinges, a strong metallic odor hit her nostrils. It reminded her of the sweaty workout equipment at the gym. When the door swung open, her jaw dropped at the sight inside.

Her son's bed was occupied by the two women from the previous night. The mattress was stained red with blood, as were their naked bodies. The sheets and bedspread lay twisted on the floor at the foot of the bed. Emerging from within the tangled covers, Jessica saw an arm and part of a leg, both also covered with blood. Her legs weakened, almost giving out at the realization. Her son's dead body lay in the discarded heap of covers on the floor. The ladies had pushed his corpse off after they were done with him and continued their tryst.

In the other bed lay two women, also naked except for the dried blood smeared across both bodies. One, unknown to Jessica, but clearly a relation of the two sisters in her son's bed and the other, her daughter Ashley.

Jessica took a step inside the room to see if, by any chance, her daughter was alive. As her worst fears became realized, a distant scream filled the room. Time moved in slow motion. Each blink of her eyes was like the next frame of an old film. She closed her mouth and the screaming stopped. Turning to her husband, their eyes locked. She saw a look of horror and fear on his face. It wasn't until his body started shaking did she see Marius standing behind David. His grin was feral, revealing fangs as sharp as needles. Marius's glistening teeth sank deeply into her husband's neck. Blood sprayed from the gash like a fountain.

Jessica's eyes locked with David's. He tried to speak but could only mouth the word "Go."

Jessica's survival instincts kicked in. She pushed past her dying husband into the hallway and ran. The castle's long corridors had many turns and Jessica had not been through most of them. Keeping to what she knew, Jessica ran towards the courtyard and headed directly for the exit. She burst through the doors, into the morning sunlight. Taking a quick look back over her shoulder, she was surprised Marius had made no attempt to follow her.

Scurrying through the courtyard, she eyed the large gate on the far end. As far as she knew, this was the only exit from the castle. When Jessica reached the gate, she pushed it with all her might, but it did not budge. She scanned the nearby area for a way to open it. A locking mechanism sat on the wall to the right of the gate. She took a few quick steps over to it and took hold of the lever. The cold metal of the handle sent goosebumps up her arm. The first pull moved it halfway down and with another good tug, the locking mechanism on the gate made a loud click. Jessica pushed the gate, and it swung open. She stepped forward with the door, but stopped herself just as she was about to fall over the edge of the threshold. Her foot knocked a loose stone, which tumbled down off the path to a large drop below.

Her stomach sank. To Jessica's surprise, the drawbridge, though out of service, had been raised. She had no way to escape except a twenty-five foot drop.

Looking back to the castle entrance, she wondered why Marius hadn't followed. It reminded her of the horror movies Jeremy made her sit through. Vampires can't go into direct sunlight. Still unwilling to believe vampires are real, she thought maybe these were just psychos who acted like vampires. Either way, she didn't want to stick around to find out. If the sun did protect her, that would only keep her safe for so long. Not seeing any other option, she looked down at the grassy hill below. She leaped, hoping to roll with her fall, but instead landed feet first. The impact was more than her bones could handle. Jessica knew her ankles were broken by the sound. Both of them shattered upon impact with a loud crunching sound. She didn't need to see the bone that protruded from each leg to know, she'd have no hope of walking. She fell to her knees and rolled a few feet before coming to a rest on her back. Her stare fixed up towards the large stone pillar which should have held the drawbridge for her escape.

Jessica lay on her back, panting. Immense pain shot up both of her legs as she gazed at the sky. Her thoughts of how to escape with two broken ankles became silenced by a deep growl as a long gray snout came into view. The growling increased as more furry faces clouded her vision until she could no longer see the sky, just sharp, hungry teeth. The wolves encircled her, pushing closer until she could barely breathe. Gasping for air, she could only smell the wolves' sour breath. Hysterical from her current situation, Jessica hummed a nursery rhyme to herself. As the wolves closed in and bit into her flesh, the last thought through her mind... *Oh my, what sharp teeth you have. They look just like the ones that ate my husband.*

Free Lunch

Asheville, NC
2014

Jeff Gallo strolled into work for another day at the grind. Working for a local tech startup for the past five years had been a labor of love. Although at first he felt overworked and underpaid, the company had expanded significantly over the years. During Jeff's first days at FitFriend, the company employed only twenty people but has since grown to over one hundred and fifty employees. After climbing up the corporate ladder through a few promotions, he felt well compensated for his work as a software developer. During that time, the company launched a new social media platform for fitness enthusiasts to help friends keep each other motivated. Jeff had been the lead programmer for the backend of the site, and the launch brought a lot of good press for the company, which wouldn't have gone nearly as smoothly without Jeff's coding skills.

Passing by the front desk, he gave the receptionist a wave as he grabbed a hard candy from the dish on her desk. She glanced up at him with a smile and nod, then went back to her screen. Turning the corner to walk down the hall, Jeff noticed a game of solitaire on her monitor. Before heading to his cube, Jeff had a routine of stopping by the kitchen area first to drop off his lunch or at least pretend to drop off his lunch on the days he didn't bring one. The route from the kitchen back to his desk would take him through the marketing area. That's where Sarah Grant sat. Sarah was a marketing something-or-other with dirty blonde hair, a perfect smile and protruding eyes that Jeff often had to stop himself from getting lost in. He'd prefer to avoid being labeled as the office creep. Jeff had a crush on her for a year, ever since her first day with the company. Seeing her on his way in before getting started brought a smile to Jeff's face and, for him, was the equivalent of most people's morning cup of coffee. Even if on most days he only saw the back of her head, since she was often already typing away with her headphones on. Just smelling the air as he walked by Sarah's cube helped open his eyes and get his blood pumping.

Sitting down at his desk, Jeff booted up his computer and brought up his current project, setting up a new database for the website. After only a few minutes of working, a notification lit up the corner of Jeff's computer. The title of the incoming email caught his eye. The subject line read 'Free Pizza'. Switching from his coding program over to *Outlook*, he clicked on the new message. The email was from Debbie, the human resources assistant. After scanning it quickly, he muttered to himself, "Ahh, I knew it. There's always a catch."

The large graphic at the top of the email displayed a 3D smiling heart holding a slice of pizza with a curved red line leading to what looked like an icon of a medical bag half filled with blood. Below the graphic in a large typeface:

DONATE BLOOD, SAVE A LIFE
Free Pizza For All Donors
Tuesday, March 24th 12-4pm
Sign up now by the reception desk
Sponsored by RedLife Corp.

Jeff never passed up free food, but the thought of a needle in his arm sent a chill down his spine. At his most recent doctor's appointment, the nurse drew blood for testing. On his way out, Jeff fainted right in front of a horrified little girl with her mother. Out of embarrassment, he's avoided the doctor's office ever since.

The donation time in the middle of the workday was enticing, since he'd be on the clock for the procedure. Maybe this would give him an excuse to head home early if he felt nauseous after the appointment. He'd never given blood before and wasn't ready to commit, but what's the worst that could happen? The blood drive was still almost a week away, so he had time to decide. The bottom of the email recommended an appointment, but noted they often have space for walk-ins. If they booked up and he missed his chance, he sure wouldn't lose any sleep over it. Switching back to his programming software, Jeff scanned the function he had been working on to find his place and went back to editing the code.

A few days later, on Jeff's way into the office, he passed by the front desk and noticed the sign-up sheet for the blood drive. At the top of the page sat the same eye-catching graphic of the red heart with a big, shit-eating grin on its face while pumping blood into the nearby bag. Scanning the sheet quickly, he saw almost half the spaces were full, but one name stuck out immediately: Sarah Grant. Sarah's name occupied a 2pm time slot and one other 2pm slot remained open. Thanking his lucky stars and not being one to miss a chance at having some quality time to chat up his crush for an hour, Jeff scribbled his name on the other 2pm line. If he fainted from the blood loss, maybe Sarah would give him CPR. Not likely, but he can dream.

The following Tuesday came, and Jeff's mind raced with the prospect of spending time with Sarah that afternoon. He checked the sign-up sheet again to make sure she hadn't canceled or changed her spot. The sheet only had a few openings remaining. He relaxed upon seeing their names still next to each other. This time, on passing Sarah's cube, he stopped by to mention their 'date' that afternoon. Her music played loud enough to hear *Mumford and Sons* as he approached. Not his typical tunes, but he could easily look past the difference in musical taste.

A wind-up set of chattering teeth stood on the desk next to a giraffe beanie baby. Pictures of family or friends adorned the walls of her cube, intermixed with various bumper stickers and inspirational quotes. She had a whole other life that Jeff knew almost nothing about. Maybe one day he would be lucky enough to be in one of the pictures.

Since her music played at near top volume, he gave Sarah a quick tap on the shoulder to let her know of his presence. She jumped in her seat, hands going straight to her headphones.

She spun around, slipped them off and glanced at Jeff. "Oh my God, you almost gave me a heart attack!" she said.

"Sorry about that," he replied with a grin. "I was just stopping by because I saw we're scheduled to donate blood at the same time today. I wanted to remind you to have a big lunch and keep your sugar level up."

Sarah giggled at the warning. She said, "Oh, this isn't my first rodeo. I donate regularly, so it's no problem for me. Have you donated before?"

"Actually, this is my first time. I guess that makes me a virgin. I might need someone to hold my hand," Jeff said with a nervous laugh.

Sarah blushed. She knew Jeff had a thing for her. He was a little geeky compared to her usual type, but he was funny and cute, so she would consider a date... *if* he ever got around to asking her out. "Oh really, well I'm happy to be there while you get your cherry popped. It's no big deal. It'll be over before you know it, and it's for a noble cause," she said, rolling her chair closer to Jeff and giving him a flirtatious nudge.

With that, they both laughed again and had an awkward silence. "Well, I guess I'll see you in a couple hours," Jeff said, and he turned to head back to his cube.

The blood extraction took place in the office parking lot in a mobile medical van. Jeff approached the van cautiously. It looked like a white armored truck, with the only difference being the letters spelling out *RedLife* and that same damn smiling heart logo again. Entering the vehicle, Jeff noticed the pristine condition of everything inside. The van seemed like it had just rolled off the showroom floor. Inside the van, two nurses scurried about, one of them already attending to Sarah, who sat in a padded chair with her sleeve rolled up. The nurse finished inserting the needle into her arm, taking no notice of Jeff. The other nurse greeted him and motioned for him to sit next to Sarah. He sat on the medical chair, making a loud crunching sound from the exam paper that lined the seat. He leaned back and rolled up his sleeve in preparation. A bead of sweat rolled down the side of his cheek.

Sarah saw the look on Jeff's face as he exposed his arm. "Take it easy on him. He's a first timer," she told the nurses.

Even though Sarah made the comment in jest, Jeff was glad to have that out there without having to seem like a wimp by bringing it up himself. Maybe sitting next to Sarah put him at ease or maybe he was trying to act macho in front of her, but either way, the process itself proved easier than Jeff expected.

The nurse who had been helping Sarah came over to him and inserted the cannula into his arm, finding a suitable vein effortlessly. She had a passive demeanor, showing almost no emotion, but everything about her was professional. After a quick pinch and what felt like just a few minutes of flirting with Sarah, the nurse unhooked the tubes and removed the needle from his arm.

"Oh, that's it?" Jeff asked, surprised it was over so quickly. "I feel like I could give more."

The nurse smiled. "We'd love to draw more from you, but unfortunately, that's all we can take today. We have you on our mailing list now, so you'll be hearing from us soon." She winked at him before unhooking the freshly drawn blood bag and storing it in a refrigerator with a dozen other bags.

Throughout the years, vampires have had many willing donors, but once they figured out how to pull the wool over the sheep's eyes by taking control of the blood donation industry, vampires flourished like never before. Instead of slinking around back alleys or prowling for drunks at the local pubs, they now sat in office and medical buildings throughout the world.

By distributing sustenance to the vampire population, they no longer had to take lives and deal with the consequences. It became easier to fly under the radar. Sure, the primal urge that came with being an apex predator was hard to suppress, but vampires were smart and the prospect of long-term survival with delivery service often outweighed a quick bite.

There have been too many close calls throughout history, requiring massive cover-ups to conceal the truth from the public. Creating natural disasters and staging world wars does not come cheap. The rise of video capture technology had further complicated their struggle to stay hidden, but luckily so far the leaks that made it to the internet had been chalked up to doctored videos and special effects.

Phillip Maier paced back and forth behind the row of computers as he looked at the graphs displayed on the monitors. As the CEO of RedLife Corp, he had an enormous responsibility. Not just to the company as a normal CEO would, but his duties also included feeding his entire species. If you think Karen at your local fast-food joint is hangry, you've never seen a vampire that's gone a week without a blood pack. Making sure his brethren didn't step out of line and bring prying eyes into their community was his sister company's job, and they did a damn good job of it, but satiated vampires were much easier to keep in check. Needless to say, the two companies worked hand-in-hand in nearly all matters.

At every workstation Phillip passed, sat a data technician diligently watching the information flow across the multiple displays in front of them. Wearing headsets, their eyes darted back and forth between screens. The row of monitors showed real-time data of all the blood being collected around the globe. Sensors in the extraction process transmitted the data back to RedLife's main server. The information populated their proprietary database with all the medical information they would need to ensure vampires across the world have a never ending food supply. RedLife's database included not only blood types but also samples of the donors' DNA and metadata, as well as any current or future health problems that may arise. RedLife had an image to uphold, which meant distributing only the highest quality product. The collection process separated the rarer blood types, which could fetch high prices from the vampire aristocrats.

As Philip continued his rounds, he heard a workstation emit a beeping notification. He stopped and turned to check the monitor and he saw a pop up on the screen.

The employee at that station pressed a button on her headset and spoke into the mic, "Hello, we just scanned a suitable candidate for the open position in our technology department.... Uhmm, let me see, Jeff Gallo, a computer engineer from Asheville, North Carolina. He shows some promise based on the work he's done and his blood type is compatible... No, the database says he lives alone, no girlfriend or roommate. Family lives on the other side of the country. He only sees them about once a year... Yup, OK, I'm sending the info over to you now, thanks." The technician tapped the button on her headset again to disconnect the call and pressed a few keys on the computer to transfer the info to headquarters.

A faint smile cracked on Philip's face. He enjoyed watching the system at work, and he was always eager to welcome new brethren to the company. Not all employees of RedLife needed to be turned, but certain positions required access to confidential information. Things that would raise the eyebrows of an average human and have them asking the wrong questions. The position that needed to be filled at the moment would work on the software controlling the blood distribution network. Considering only 10% of the blood they received from donors arrived at hospitals for human use, it would be tough to explain where the rest went.

Of course, Philip hated giving 10% of their blood back to the humans, but it was necessary to keep up appearances. It remained difficult enough to hide the true destinations of the lion's share of shipments, but installing vampire loyalists in the right government positions throughout the world had helped keep a lid on their operation.

Early the next morning, Jeff's nightstand buzzed from the vibration on his phone which played *Five Finger Death Punch,* his default ringtone. Jeff turned over in bed to silence the phone. He checked the caller ID. It displayed RedLife Corp. Strange; he thought to himself, why would they be calling at this hour? Probably an automated 'thank you for donating' call. He let it go to voicemail and rolled back over to doze a few more minutes before getting ready for the day. Ten minutes later, the phone rang again. This time, awake in bed and knowing he had to be getting up soon anyway, he answered.

"Hello, may I please speak with Jeff Gallo?" the young lady on the other end asked and then after confirming it was him, "I'm sorry to tell you this, but we noticed an anomaly in the blood we took yesterday. We need you to come to the lab for some follow-up testing as soon as possible."

"What kind of anomaly? What do you mean?" he asked.

"Well, it's nothing to be too concerned about, but we would prefer it if you came in for another test and to speak with one of our doctors so they can answer any questions you have. You don't need an appointment. Just head on down to our lab and we'll see you soon. Thanks."

Jeff sent a quick email to his boss, letting him know he had to go to the doctor's office and would be late to work. With no meetings scheduled for the morning, heading to the lab first thing was no issue. Everyone at the office knows Jeff is a reliable worker and FitFriend is always accommodating when personal matters come up. Regardless of the operator's comment about nothing to worry about, Jeff felt uneasy about the office visit. He took a quick shower and put on jeans and a t-shirt, his normal business attire, and rushed out the door. He hopped in his car and headed to the address the caller had given him to learn more about this anomaly.

RedLife's blood lab was located on the basement level of a brick building in a tech park that housed various medical offices. Upon entering the lab, the receptionist glanced up and greeted him as he walked over to her desk. She looked to be in her late 20s with straight auburn hair that came to the bottom of her ears. Her outfit seemed more like a traditional vintage nurse's outfit instead of the scrubs you see them wearing today. Jeff found her attire peculiar considering her young age, but he admitted it looked quite good. She had a charm in her smile that helped put Jeff at ease as he approached the desk. No one sat in the waiting area, which lacked the usual amenities such as a TV, magazines, or games. He realized he hadn't noticed anyone on the way into the building either, but chalked it up to the early hour of his arrival.

"You must be Mr. Gallo," said the young woman at the desk with no need for Jeff to introduce himself. She pressed a button on her switchboard and added, "The doctor will be right with you."

Before Jeff had a chance to sit down, a man in a lab coat came through the door that led to the back room. "Hi Mr. Gallo, I'm Doctor Freeman. Please follow me to the first room on your left, and we'll get started."

"Get started with what? I'm not even sure why I'm here," Jeff asked.

"Oh, I'm sorry. We just need to draw a small amount of blood for testing. Much less than you donated yesterday, so it should be no trouble. We can discuss the details of the matter in the exam room."

The examination room looked like it belonged in a science lab rather than a doctor's office. All types of instruments and equipment filled the room. Next to the chair sat a tray with an array of medical tools spread out, including a few vials of various substances. Dr. Freeman noticed Jeff eyeing the instruments nervously and tried to relieve his anxiety, saying, "Oh, don't worry about those, just standard stuff. We won't even be using all of it."

Then, in a flash, before Jeff realized what was happening, the doctor had a syringe in his hand. Moving uncannily fast, the doctor plunged the syringe deep into Jeff's neck as the white fluid within emptied from the chamber. Jeff tried to get up with a yell, but the doctor's hand was firmly pressing against his chest with an unnatural strength. He struggled, but as he fought, Jeff could feel his strength waning. The lights in the room dimmed and a wave of nausea rose from his stomach as he felt the walls closing in.

The next thing Jeff knew, he opened his eyes from a slumber, feeling groggy, but immediately remembering the events that preceded his sudden nap. He tried to stand, but was unable. At first, he thought his muscles had yet to recover, but soon noticed the straps binding his wrists and ankles to the chair. Powerless to move, his gaze panned across the room until he spotted the doctor, who stood in the corner watching Jeff's arousal.

"Welcome back to the land of the living, Mr. Gallo. Even if, technically, it is for the last time," said the doctor. "But don't let that scare you. You'll have many years left on this earth. I know you don't have a clue what I'm talking about, but be patient. I can't wait to explain everything to you." A genuine look of joy spreading across his face.

The doctor stepped closer to Jeff, holding another syringe in his hand, this one filled with a dark red fluid. Jeff started convulsing as the doctor approached. He struggled in vain to prevent the inevitable. Between the straps and the doctor's strength, his attempts at thwarting the man's advance were futile.

"What are you doing? Get away from me!" Jeff shouted as the man took hold of his neck and stretched it, exposing a swath of flesh.

"This will be easier for everyone if you try to relax. I'm just going to inject you with some of my blood. It won't quite kill you, and it will open up a whole new world you never knew existed." With that, he drove the second syringe into Jeff's neck. The vampire blood inside the syringe slowly transferred into Jeff's bloodstream. The veins around the injection site throbbed and turned a deep shade of purple, extending in a spiderweb effect.

"What did you just do to me? What is happening?" Jeff yelled as the pain from the injection coursed through his body. He struggled against the straps that held him, but they did not give. The materials used could withstand much more than his strength could muster.

"Over the next 24 hours you will die and leave your old life behind, only to be reborn as something… greater. I will not sugarcoat it. This transformation will be painful, but in the end, you will join us at the top of the food chain." Dr. Freeman continued to explain to Jeff about the transition and his new life. The doctor knew Jeff didn't believe a word he said. None of them ever did, but soon enough, the transformation would be complete and once Jeff felt the hunger for himself, he would surely understand. After his first feeding, Jeff's emotional attachment to his old life will fade and a few days of mentoring will complete his assimilation. The assimilation process had been honed over the years, and most vampires adjusted to their new lives rather easily. Another proud point for Phillip during his time as CEO.

After extending his sick leave through the rest of the week, the following Monday, Jeff returned to work. This time, when arriving at the office, instead of his morning ritual through the marketing area, he went straight to his boss's office. Jeff knocked on the open door and entered with his official letter of resignation in his hand. The letter spelled out his last day working for FitFriend would be in two weeks. His boss knew Jeff enjoyed the job and was surprised when Jeff presented him with the letter. However, no amount of pleading or offers of a salary increase could get Jeff to change his mind. Jeff had accepted a new position at RedLife as a Senior Software Developer and although he had no desire to fulfill these final two weeks at FitFriend, a remnant of a life he was eager to leave behind, his new superiors were adamant that he complete this final act of office etiquette. After all, vampires were nothing, if not civilized.

Although he still had urges for Sarah, they were now both sexual and predatory. Jeff was not sure he could control himself in the heat of the moment, and his new brothers had been very clear about consequences for attacking or killing a human. Part of his initiation included watching an uncooperative vampire's execution for a midnight feeding that left a girl dead. It was explained to the new vampires that punishing their own kind was not something they enjoyed, but it was a necessary evil for the greater good of their species. The condemned vampire was brought into a circular area that resembled an indoor gladiator arena and chained to a wooden cross. Then a retractable roof opened and sunlight poured down into the room. Almost immediately, a trail of smoke emanated from the vampire's exposed skin. The epidermis sizzled and, within a few seconds, portions of its body dissolved in on itself. The creature let out a blood-curdling scream of death. The cry continued until his gaping throat could no longer push out the air required to yell. Less than 30 seconds from when the first rays of light came down, a pile of ash and bone was all that remained.

Jeff, along with three other newborn vampires, saw this spectacle first hand sitting in what most closely resembled movie theater chairs. The only thing missing was the popcorn. Tucked safely behind a specialized tempered glass window, wearing custom Ray-Ban sunglasses, the new vampires watched one of their kind exit this world forever.

Jeff still wore those same sunglasses when he pulled his car into the office parking garage that morning. The glasses were for show, but the vampires had outfitted his car with the same protective glass windows as the viewing room, allowing him to travel freely during the day as long as his destination had a safely enclosed garage to park in. The conveniences of modern technology have greatly improved the average vampire's quality of life.

Word of Jeff's imminent departure from the company spread quickly through the gossip train. When Sarah heard he was leaving, she became disheartened but also hopeful. She'd grown to enjoy his friendship, but maybe this would give them the opportunity for something more. While many had no qualms about dating a coworker, others preferred not to mix business and pleasure, since it could lead to awkward interactions if things didn't work out. Sarah was well aware of Jeff's 'morning routine' of walking by her desk and considered it cute, in a stalkery way, so she became confused when he suddenly stopped. Instead, she tried to strike up a conversation with him about his new job, but to her surprise and dismay, he blew her off. Sarah thought his new behavior was odd, and didn't enjoy being rejected, but she wasn't one to beg.

Back at his desk, Jeff found it hard to concentrate on work. His heightened senses still reeling from the new sensations he felt. Sarah was the last thing on his mind. His brain raced with anticipation for what lay ahead in his new job and new life. His eyes watched the clock while he waited for the end of the day. Jeff's thirst returned and he couldn't wait to get some more of those delicious blood packs.

Blood Spotters

W orld Wide Web
2024

Transcription of Blood Spotters Podcast, Episode 12

Jerry: Hello and welcome to another episode of *Blood Spotters*, the internet's #1 vampire podcast! This is your host Jerry, and I'm here with

Steve: Steve! And we've got another great show for you today.

Jerry: On this episode we're going to do a deep-dive into the history of vampires. A legend as pervasive around the world as this must have some truth to its origin, right?

Steve: Most definitely, Jerry. Vampires go way back. Most people think of Dracula or Nosferatu as the first vampire, but those stories are just a couple hundred years old. Vampires appear in legends and folklore going back thousands of years.

Jerry: That's right Steve, and they don't all just come from one culture either. These legends are virtually the same from all over the world. The coincidences are too big to ignore. Just to run through a few of the earliest legends. Old Norse Mythology speaks of Draugr– animated corpses, also referred to as 'ghosts with bodies' that rose from the grave with a lust for blood. The Draugr were also known to control the weather and shape-shift into various animals. Are you noticing the similarities yet?

Steve: You know, some people even say the Native American Wendigo were vampires. The indigenous legends speak of a creature that once was human. The corrupted monster looks like a man with a foul stench and a heart of ice. And, of course, it feasted on human flesh and blood.

Jerry: Here's one of my favorite examples, Steve. Just a few decades ago, archeologists found a mass grave near Yorkshire, England. The bodies were from a medieval town named Wharram Percy. This village turned into a ghost town. No one knew what happened, but all the residents disappeared, virtually overnight.

Steve: Sounds strange, but that can't be the whole story. What sort of evidence linked the town to vampires?

Jerry: Just recently, archeologists uncovered a mass grave in the town. They excavated something like over one hundred and fifty bones from the site. All the bodies had been dismembered and even weirder, someone had smashed in the front of the skulls, breaking all of their teeth. Examination of the bones determined that the desecration of the skulls came after the subjects were already deceased.

Steve: Ok, that sounds a bit extra. How old was the grave?

Jerry: Yeah, it's pretty wild. The bones had been burned as well, so analyzing them took a while. Carbon dating estimated the bones to be about a thousand years old.

Steve: Wow, that makes Dracula look like a baby! So when did people start realizing these myths and legends from around the world might be the same type of creature?

Jerry: Well, by the 17th century, reports of vampires out of Serbia, Croatia, France, Prussia, Hungary and Transylvania, just to name a few, had been piling up. At that time, the belief in vampires across Europe and much of Asia was widely accepted as fact. Although at that point, each culture had its own name for the phenomenon. It wasn't until the early 18th century, that medical professionals who had been studying the affliction and working to reverse the effects coined the term 'vampir'. Remember, this is almost 200 years before Bram Stoker wrote *Dracula*.

Steve: Speaking of old, don't forget about Sekhmet. Some consider her the first known vampire in the world. She was a fierce warrior goddess in ancient Egypt. Fighting enemies of Ra, the sun god, she went into a frenzy during battle, killing everyone and everything in her path. It is said the only way to stop her destruction was for her to drink the blood of her enemies.

Jerry: Wicked. It makes you wonder about the origins of it. Is it some kind of disease or virus? If it is, maybe we can come up with a cure or even a vaccination. And if scientists were working on this so long ago, where are the results? Why isn't this more common knowledge? With today's advancements in science and technology, we should have eradicated these fuckers by now.

Steve: The obvious answer to that one, Jerry, is the scientists probably all got themselves killed or turned into vampires. If any of our fans out there have thoughts about the origins of vampirism or any scientific knowledge of the disease, we'd love to hear from you.

Jerry: We could be here all night, going into detail on hundreds of these instances from all over the world, but I don't want to bore you with too much of a history lesson, so let's take a few calls from our listeners.

Jerry: Caller #1 you're on the air.

Caller #1: Hey guys, love the show and everything you do. My question is, if hundreds of years ago, everyone knew vampires existed, what changed for people to stop believing in them?

Steve: Wait a minute now. Not everyone stopped believing. You're talking to two true believers right here and I'm guessing you trust the evidence that's all around us as well.

Caller #1: Yeah, but you know what I mean. We are the outliers. Most people laugh us out of the room if we tell them vampires are real.

Steve: Sorry buddy, I was just having a little fun. I know what you mean.

Jerry: That is a good question, and we have some theories. But, it's hard to know what went through people's minds so long ago. It's not like they're still around today to ask.

Caller #1: The vampires may be. You could always ask them.

(laughter)

Steve: That's true, but for some reason, I don't think they would be willing to sit down for an interview.

Jerry: Honestly, I think the change in people's beliefs had to do with the rise in popularity of fictitious vampire stories like *The Vampyre* and *Dracula*. It's almost like the vampires knew they could change the narrative by associating themselves with works of fiction instead of medical enigmas. After all, everyone knows monster movie horrors couldn't possibly be real.

Caller #1: So, are you saying Bram Stoker was a vampire?

Steve: It's definitely not outside the realm of possibility.

Jerry: If you ask me, I think the vampires are controlling everything; Hollywood, the government, the media, Wall Street. They have enough money and power to silence anyone who learns the truth.

Caller #1: So, if they silence anyone who knows the truth and here you are spouting off all their secrets, why are you still alive?

(nervous laughter)

Jerry: Ok, next caller.

Caller #2: Hello, I'm calling because I'm concerned about my son. I'm worried that he is a vampire. He sleeps all day and never leaves the house. His only friends are on that stupid computer. He just stays in the basement and is up all night playing those silly video games. It's such a waste of time, and I'm sure it has melted his brain.

Jerry: Steve, maybe you should take this one. You seem to have a lot in common with this guy.

Steve: Har har har. Listen lady, your son sounds more like a zombie than a vampire and that's not really in our wheelhouse. But all jokes aside, that's pretty much normal behavior for kids these days. We love a good conspiracy theory, and it doesn't take much to convince us, but we need a little more than that to go on.

Caller #2: If you could hear that god-awful music he listens to, you would see. It's all screaming and noise. I tell you, it's devil music! The only time he even leaves the basement is when he's eating all of my food.

Jerry: Hold up, eating your food? You realize vampires don't eat food; they drink blood.

Caller #2: Uhhhhh, well....

Steve: It sounds to me like you have yourself a normal teenager, next caller.

Caller #3: Heyyy, long-time fan, first time caller. I just want to say that I LOVE YOU STEVE!! Will you marry me?

Steve: Awww, thanks dear. I love you too, but I'm sorry to say that if we were to be married, it would put you in too much danger. I could never live with myself if something bad happened to you.

Jerry: Steve the heartbreaker. Let 'em down easy, my man!

Steve: That being said honey, if you want to leave me with your number, I'd be happy to give you a ring next time I'm passing through your city. I never like to disappoint my fans.

Jerry: You sly dog. One of these days, you better tell me your secret. Anyway, I think that's about all the time we have for today. We'll catch you next time on

Jerry & Steve: Blood Spotters!

Transcription of Blood Spotters Podcast, Episode 13

Jerry: Good morning Blood Spotters, this is Jerry back with another live episode and I'm really excited about our show today. We have an extra special guest who is going to drop a bombshell on us. For his own safety, we won't use his real name, but we're gonna call him Joe. Joe is a technician at RedLife Corp.

Steve: You know RedLife, the largest private blood donation and transfusion company in the world.

Jerry: I'm sure you've seen their smiling heart logo before. It's plastered all over their ads and transport vehicles.

Steve: Anyway... he says the entire place is run by vampires! But I don't want to steal too much of his thunder, so we'll let you hear it straight from the horse's mouth, so to speak. Hey, Joe, you're live on-the-air with Blood Spotters and we're so glad you came forward. It must take a lot of guts to go public with this type of information.

Joe: Thanks for having me guys. If I'm going to be honest, I didn't really have anywhere else to turn. I saw something strange in the lab, and then I received an email from my boss about a mandatory health screening. My buddy had the health screening last week and ever since, I don't know, something's off about him. He's not the same person he used to be. I can feel it. I tried to go to the police, but they laughed me out of the building. Anyway, I'm really scared. I think I'm in serious danger.

Jerry: That doesn't sound good. I hope they didn't follow you. Are you sure you're in a secure location?

Steve: Calm down, Jerry, we don't want to spook him. I'm sure you're fine, Joe.

Jerry: Ok, Ok, I was just trying to build up some suspense.

Steve: Joe, tell us what you know about the vampires at RedLife. What tipped you off?

Joe: I've worked there as a lab technician for a few years and there have always been some weird quirks about the place since the beginning. I mean, everyone works in two shifts, half the people only come in at night.

Steve: Well, that seems pretty normal for a round the clock medical lab to me.

Joe: I don't think I even saw the people working on the other shift for the first year I was there. Anyway, that's not everything. Not even close. There are entire sections of the building that are off limits for certain people. I know what you're going to say. That's also normal for employees to have different clearance levels, but this isn't some top secret military facility. We're just a nonprofit blood organization. Every time I think I'm going to get promoted and given more access, they bring in a new outside hire. Most of these guys they bring in... yikes. Serious creep vibes.

Steve: Joe, I'm sorry to interrupt, but are you just disgruntled for being passed over on a promotion? That's what this sounds like to me.

Joe: No, no, that's not it. I mean, sure, at first I was pissed, but after what I know now, I wouldn't want a promotion. Hell, I never want to step foot inside that place again. Listen to this. One of my duties is to spot check the incoming blood. You know, to ensure it's clean and everything is good to go. Anyway, last week there was this mix-up with the vials and the blood I tested… wow. The blood was thick and clotted in this weird way. I've never seen anything like it. When I looked at the blood under a microscope, the cells were misshapen and clinging to each other. They were exhibiting very odd behavior. It was like the cells were trying to absorb each other. I almost said something to my boss but thought better of it, so I just went about my business, pretending I hadn't seen it. Then, a few minutes later, this guy from the other lab barges into the room. He finds the vials and asks me about them. I told him I'd been backed up all day and hadn't looked at it yet. He seemed really relieved when I told him that and then took the vials out of the room, down the hall, to one of the restricted rooms.

Jerry: Wow, that sounds pretty heavy. You must have been nervous. Quick thinking pretending you hadn't looked at it yet. But you know, coming on this show, there's a chance they might hear this and figure out who you are. We take our guests' safety with the utmost concern, but there's only so much we can do to protect you.

Joe: Thank you, but I think that ship has sailed. I knew my lie would only buy me some time. They have cameras everywhere and would see the truth soon enough. I got out of there as fast as I could, and luckily, I still had the sample I examined.

Steve: Hold up! Are you telling me you have real life vampire blood in your possession?

Joe: Yes, and I am happy to share my findings with anyone who will listen.

Jerry: That's great, but just to play devil's advocate here. You found some experimental blood that you weren't supposed to see. What made you think it was vampire blood?

Joe: Well, as soon as I got home, I looked at the sample again in a microscope when I had more time to examine it. This blood... I've never seen anything like it. Half of the cells were dead, but they still had properties of active cells. With more time to study the blood, I set up a time lapse video. This is the real kicker. When I sped up the playback and watched the video, I saw those deformed cells attach themselves to the normal cells and I don't really know how to explain it. The diseased cell just kind of ate the healthy cell. It was so strange; I did a few internet searches for what could cause this. That's when I found some forum posts on vampirism and the constant need to consume human blood. Then I found a link to your podcast, and I ended up listening to your show. You guys really made a lot of sense to me after everything I'd seen and gave me a feeling that maybe I wasn't alone in this.

Jerry: Well thanks, that means a lot and I promise you, we are with you 'till the end. We've dedicated our lives to getting the truth out to as many people as we can before it's too late.

Steve: And you said you took this news to the police? If this conspiracy goes as far as you say it does, didn't it cross your mind that the police are probably already in on it?

Joe: It's funny you say that because the detective I talked to acted like he took me seriously, but on my way out, I heard him laughing about it with his buddies. They took me for a kook, but this one guy... I could feel his eyes on me as I left and I don't know, he just gave me the freaking willies. Something was off about him. Still though, after the way the cops laughed at me, they had me second guessing if I wasn't just going crazy. So I left the station, and I'm on my way home when I get this notification from my security system. I bring up my camera feed and those fuckers were in my house!

Jerry: No way, who?

Joe: A security team from the lab. Luckily, I brought the blood sample with me, but I had the video captured on my computer and I'm sure they found it. At that point I didn't know where to go, but I thought of a place to hide out for a while, and that's when I called you guys.

Steve: Wow Joe, that's some heavy shit for you to just drop on us like that. Don't worry, we'll help spread your proof far and wide. After the show's over, we'll chat about where we can meet and bring you back to our safe-house.

Jerry: Is that what you're calling your mom's basement these days, Steve?

Steve: Ha ha Jerry. Anyway, we're going to sign off now and link up with Joe. We'll be back next episode with a closer look at the evidence against RedLife Corp. from our inside source.

Transcription of Blood Spotters Podcast, Episode 14

Steve: Hey guys, this is so fucked. Sorry we're late with this broadcast, but some crazy shit has been going down. Joe from RedLife never showed up for our rendezvous. We didn't know if he got scared and ran, or if the vampires got to him. Either scenario is just as likely. So we waited a while and then went back to the studio to get ready for the show without him.

Jerry: The show must go on!

Steve: That's right, but just as we were about to start, some sketchy vans pulled up outside. They must have followed us from the rendezvous.

Jerry: Luckily, we have this place outfitted with cameras and saw them coming a mile away.

Steve: We escaped out the side before they got in, but they trashed all of our equipment and destroyed most of our research.

Jerry: It seems like our last segment on RedLife Corp. really struck a nerve and they tried to silence us. But we can't be silenced!

Steve: That's right Jerry, we can't be silenced. We're coming to you from an undisclosed backup studio that we had ready in case something like this happened.

Jerry: The best part of all is that we're not even mad. Now we have the proof we need to blow this whole thing open. Even without Joe's blood sample.

Steve: We do hope our friend Joe is okay. But as for our studio, we have surveillance footage of those bloodsuckers destroying our equipment, and we left a little surprise for them in case they found us. We're uploading the video now, so head on over to our YouTube channel for irrefutable proof of the vampire conspiracy.

Transcription of Blood Spotters Podcast, Episode 15 (final broadcast)

Jerry: Holy shit guys. I'm sure everyone knows by now, and I hate to say it, but we were right. Turn on the news, look out the fucking window! The vampires are here. It's not safe. We need to organize. Where's the military? The national guard? Anything!? Guys, I don't know how to tell you this, so I'll just say it. Steve is dead. He didn't show up for our meeting to prep for the next show and so I headed over to his place to check on him. That's when I heard the first reports coming in on the news. It's like some sort of synchronized attack. They're everywhere. When I got to Steve's, his front door was wide open. That's never a good sign, especially in situations like this. I ran up the stairs into his house and... oh God. Steve. There he was, sitting on his couch, pale as a ghost.I'm going to be honest here, folks. I'm a skilled researcher and like to think of myself as a funny sidekick for the podcast, but I've never seen a dead body before. Especially seeing my best bud. It's got me shook.

After seeing that, I left straight away to go to our backup studio and started this broadcast. But after driving through downtown on the way back... I almost didn't make it. They were everywhere. I always knew there had to be a huge conspiracy. It was the only way for them to stay hidden for so long, but I never imagined there were this many of them! If you're listening to this, we just have to make it through the night. They can't come out during the day, so that will give us time to regroup and come up with a plan.Remember, your safest option is to avoid the vampires at all costs. If you have to confront one, you'll need to find a way to chop off its head or set it on fire. A stake through the heart will do the job, but you'll still need to finish it by burning the body. Regular bullets will barely slow them down. So just get somewhere secure and hunker down till the morning. This is Jerry from Blood Spotters, and I'll be here with you all night, keeping you safe with my voice. Ya know, I kind of feel like John Connor at the end of Termina...

[loud popping sound]

Oh shit. They found me; I don't know how, but they found me. The lights just...

[crashing sounds]

[screaming]

[inaudible]

[end of broadcast]

Factory Farm

L ocation Unknown
2065

I've heard stories from the elders about the time before. Did you know children used to run and play outside? They played games like tag or hide and seek with their friends. In the morning, big yellow buses picked the kids up and drove them to school. At school, the kids made new friends, and teachers taught them all sorts of things, like math, history, how to read books and even to write words of their own. The same yellow buses took the kids home in the afternoon, safe and sound. Eagerly waiting to hear about their day, their parents looked out the window, while cookies and juice sat on the counter. I heard kids really like cookies. I've never had one, so I wouldn't know. Except for the stories, of course. Momma doesn't like it when we ask her about the time before. Whenever we ask, she gets quiet and all teary-eyed. So I try not to bring it up. But the younger kids don't know any better. Some of the other adults don't mind talking about it. Sometimes they tell us about it when she's not around.

Sitting on the ground in our cages all day gets boring. But it could be worse. Luckily, we have Momma to teach us and play games with us. That helps the time pass. Plus, I have Jimmy. We're the same age, and he's been my best friend since before I can remember. Although we don't keep track of the days, we still count the seasons. I know there's four seasons in a year. That makes me about fourteen years old. Almost old enough to be moved into the adult cages. That's when they'll start taking us down the hall to the other rooms.

The vamps always chain our legs when they take us out of the cages. It's pointless considering how much faster and stronger they are. But they do it anyway. They can rip us apart with their bare hands if we try to run. I've seen it. I think the chains are just to make sure we remember who's in charge. It's not like the vamps have much to worry about from us humans. Most people just sit around in the cages like zombies all day. Sure, once in a while someone has a breakdown or goes wild, but it's not like they pose any real threat to the vamps. It's bad for morale in the cages, though. They'll usually start screaming about being slaves or cattle, and there's no point living like this. One guy kept hitting his head on the side of the cage over and over until blood covered his forehead and leaked from his nose like a faucet. He wouldn't stop until the vamps took him away. We never saw him again after that.

Momma tells the older kids what to expect when they take us, so we don't freak out when our time comes. They take the adults in small groups down a long hallway into rooms with doctors and nurses. Momma told us, when they put us in the chair, they'll tighten straps around our arms and legs to keep us still. That's so we don't get up before they're finished. She said to be ready for a sharp pinch when the needle pricks our arm. After that, they connect it to a tube that steals our blood. Momma said to just close our eyes and relax and try to go to sleep. It looks like a lot of blood, but it's not enough to kill us. The vamps need to keep us alive so we can keep making more blood for them. We're no good to them if we're dead. So like I said, it could be worse. Sometimes you gotta look on the bright side.

After a while, the vamps bring the people back to the cages and they take the next group. The blood loss weakens them but they're usually ok. Although, it's true some people don't come back at all. We take guesses about what happened to them. Maybe their bodies couldn't handle the extraction process. Or maybe they resisted, and the vamps had to deal with them. Either way, I'm sure it's nothing good. So just follow their orders and don't put up a fight. That's what I'll do. It's going to be my time soon. I can handle it. The needles don't scare me. I'm worried about Jimmy, though. He tries to be brave and act like my big brother, but I can see the fear in his eyes.

Since they can't take blood from the same people every day, they found other jobs to keep us busy in the meantime. They put most of the men to work building the great underground city. Some women work there too, but they have other uses for the women. I've never seen the city, but I've heard stories about the huge underground caverns. Each chamber looks like it goes on forever. But when you finally get to the end, a tunnel connects it to another cavern. When I hear stories from the workers, I think of ants building their nests. The oldest parts of the city dates back thousands of years. Those sections were originally underground crypts where the vamps could hide from humans and the sun. Gigantic statues carved into the walls show past vamp kings and queens. These portions are now revered as holy sites.

Ever since the vamps took control, and no longer had to hide their existence, they expanded the size of their sanctuary. Using humans as slaves allowed them to speed up construction. They also brought in better building materials. The newer sections look more like modern cities than underground crypts. They act as a place where vamps can live as comfortably as humans used to in the time before.

I guess the history books will consider the vamps a civilized species. You might say they don't sound very civilized, keeping us locked up inside these cages and draining our blood, but that depends on who you ask. Just like humans had once been a tribal species and transitioned to a more civilized lifestyle—farming livestock and shopping at the grocery store for the night's meal, vamps have done the same.

It's kind of ironic if you think about it. In the old times, humans used to bring out the pitchforks when a stray vampire would take their neighbor during the night. An entire city would go into lockdown over one missing child. Looking back, we'd give anything to go back to those times. But now that the vamps have stepped out of the shadows, there is no going back. They have ushered in a new age. Humans aren't even the ones writing the history books anymore. Hell, most of us don't even know how to write.

Momma isn't my real mom. At least, I don't think she is. I call her that because she raised me since I was little. Momma's job is to care for the kids. Well, not by herself. That would be too many for just her. We've always had a special bond though.

Whenever a new baby is born, it goes to a care center and lives in an incubator. I guess that's some kind of machine that takes care of the baby. They're like the opposite of the machines they use to take our blood. The vamps don't allow humans in the care center, other than the babies. I guess they don't trust us with their future food supply. They must have a lot of incubator machines though, since there are always a lot of new babies. The babies stay in the care center until they are old enough to live in the cages. That's usually around 2 years. Then, they put the toddlers in with the other kids. They keep the kids' cages in a separate area from the adults. They only allow a few adults in to care for the kids, like Momma. Even if she's not my real mom, she's the only mom I've ever known. She cares for me and loves me, and that's real to me.

As for the dads, well, it's not like anyone knows who the fathers are. Most are probably long gone by the time the kids are old enough to ask. Not that anyone does. It's not even worth wondering about. The vamps choose the strongest adults to breed. They get paired up and put into breeding pens. They rotate the males constantly to increase the odds of conception. It also keeps up diversity in the gene pool. In the old times, I heard people used to fall in love and get married. They had big fancy weddings, and the bride wore a beautiful white dress. All their friends and family came for a party and gave them gifts. It must have been so much fun.

Some people here might still develop feelings for each other, but it's easier not to get attached. The same goes for the babies. It's just another duty and you'll be better off forgetting them as soon as they leave your womb. For the females, being a breeder is actually one of the better jobs we can get. The vamps don't take blood from the pregnant women, so they get a break from the extractions. Although the mothers might get a break from the physical pain, they have the stress of knowing they will never raise or care for their children. Plus, they understand the horrible lives their children are born into. The breeders also have to worry about what happens if they don't get pregnant. Too many months go by without a child or even repeated miscarriages and you'll be replaced. They'll send you right to the feeding pen. Why would they keep a breeder who's not breeding? If you think it sounds heartless, it's no different from what you would do if you were in charge—what humans did when they were in charge.

Last night, they brought a new kid into the cage. He isn't a one of the toddlers from the incubation center. This boy is much older than that. I'd say he's about 10 years old. We've tried to talk to him, but he hasn't said anything. I'm not sure if he even knows how to talk. The others whisper and say he's been living outside, not in a cage like the rest of us. I've always dreamed of living outside, but after looking at him, I'm not so sure. He's real skinny. His ribs are almost poking through his chest. He's dirty and smelly too. His hair is so long, I've never seen hair like that before. It's all tangled and knotted. I wonder what kind of life he had on the outside. Seems like it must have been rough. Hopefully, he'll be able to tell us about it, eventually. Luckily for everyone, shower day is coming soon.

When you think about it, it's not so bad here after all. We get four meals a day, so we're never hungry. The food is always the same and it doesn't have much flavor, but at least it's filling. I don't really know how to describe the taste because I have nothing to compare it to. It's small, dry, and crunchy. I imagine it tastes like cookies. I close my eyes and pretend it's a warm chocolate chip cookie, just out of the oven, like in the stories.

The cages used to be really filthy, but the vamps passed new health laws regulating how they have to store humans. A lot of us were getting sick and dying from disease. I'm not sure what they expected, considering our living conditions. The tainted blood made the vamps sick, too. Now they have to test our blood to make sure we're clean, even the kids. They take away anyone with dirty blood. It's obvious what happens to them, even if we don't see it. It's probably a good thing, since the sickness would spread if the infected stayed with us in the cages. They give us a lot of shots now to help keep us clean. The little kids cry, but it doesn't bother me. The needles are good practice for when we're old enough for the extractions.

They put in a shower room because of the new rules. There isn't any privacy, but we're used to that. Plus we can wash the piss and shit off our legs. Even if we have to go stand back in it again when we're done, it's better than nothing. They have slaves clean the cages while we're gone, but they're still dirty when we return. The new showers are nice, even if the water is cold. I'm grateful they don't use the hoses to wash us anymore. They were painful and if it hit you directly, they left bruises all over your body. Spraying us down like we're some kind of circus animal was kind of humiliating. Now, each group is allowed five minutes in the shower. It's usually my favorite day of the week. Except in winter since it's so cold. They don't give us towels, so we just use our hands to wring ourselves off.

I'm glad we have short hair. Especially after seeing the new kid. It dries quicker that way. I don't want to worry about getting it knotted like him. They'll shave him soon. They shave us every season to keep away the bugs. It's one less thing for us to worry about. Since everyone has the same hair, it's normal for us.

Some of us have clothes to wear, but they are mostly just tattered rags. It would be nice to have a beautiful dress like in the stories Momma tells us. Closets full of ball gowns in every color with flowing ruffles and rhinestones. Bows for our hair and sparkling earrings. But if we had all that pretty stuff, it would just get dirty and ruined in our cages. So there's no point. At least I have my rags. Some people don't even have those. They just stand around naked all day. It's not like any of us are shy or anything, but like I mentioned, it gets cold during the winter. Momma tries to make sure the kids are taken care of. Especially the girls.

The vamps don't let us freeze to death in the cages, but the winter months are pretty bad. We spend most of our time huddled together in groups to keep warm. The body heat helps, but the winters are long. Most people find it's easier to turn their minds off and just stand in a daze. To those people, the cold helps numb their pain.

We tried talking to the new boy, but he just stared at us with these wide eyes. He only made weird grunting sounds and gestures with his hands. I guess he never learned how to talk. He must use hand signals to talk to his family. He has to have a family, right? Or at least others like him. I couldn't imagine he grew up alone. I wonder how many people live like him, on the outside? Maybe there is an entire city of humans who still live free. Like on an island somewhere. It's strange that the boy came by himself. Maybe the vamps killed his family. Or else they caught him when he was alone. Maybe his friends are searching for him right now. If they're smart they'll stay away from this place.

Anyway, it's going to be a long process to get him used to his new life in the cages. Hopefully, we can get answers from him eventually. This entire ordeal with the new boy has some of us thinking about a different way of life. There's no way for us to escape though, so it's pointless, but I guess everyone's allowed to dream. When it comes down to it, I don't think most of us could even survive out on our own. Only the elders have ever been free and there's not many of them left. The rest of us are no different from animals brought up in captivity. Unlikely to make it in the wild. They don't know how to hunt or make a shelter, anything really. Most would probably starve or freeze to death in the first week. Nevermind the fact that these blood-thirsty vamps are out there. Hiding from them would be tough enough without the added pressure of finding your next meal. Did I mention they have really good eyes, and even better ears?

This is it! They finally came for me. They took me in shackles, along with a few others my age. None of us have done this before, so we're all a little nervous. Something weird is happening, though. I'm not sure where we're going, but I don't think it's good. At least Jimmy is here with me. Everything Momma prepared us for—about the room with the machine that takes our blood. None of it is right. We walked past those rooms, up a ramp and through a large opening in the platform. We were standing in a small, dark room. After we were all inside, they pulled a metal door down from above and latched it. We stood in the dark, unsure what was happening. A minute later, we heard a rumbling that vibrated the entire room. The sound of an engine roared, and the room jerked forward. It caught us off guard and we all fell to the floor. The room kept moving, and we realized we were inside a truck. I've never been in a truck before, or any vehicle for that matter.

Everyone who comes back to the cages after the blood extraction talks about the rooms down the hall. None of them told stories of a truck. Why were we in a truck and where were we going? They take the construction workers in trucks, but they wouldn't take only a couple kids for hard labor. They need strong adults for that. Maybe there are other jobs lined up for us. That must be it. That's why some people never come back to the cages. Maybe I'll be a housemaid for a vampire princess. Wouldn't that be grand? Living in a castle, just like all the stories Momma tells us. I might not be the princess in this story, but surely living in the servant quarters would be better than being kept in a cage.

As the speed of the truck increased, bumps on the road jostled us repeatedly. After a few falls, we were smart enough to stay seated and braced against the cold metal sides of the vehicle. We couldn't help but gossip about where our journey would lead as we traveled. Our minds raced with curiosity and terror at the thought of our unknown destination. The others liked my idea of being servants for rich vampires, but their thoughts were more grim than that. Although Jimmy suggested we might be turned into vampires ourselves! That thought didn't even cross my mind. I'm not sure I like that idea either, but I'll have to think about it. Not like it's my decision, anyway.

Another fifteen minutes passed before the truck came to a stop and the engine turned off. My heart raced with anticipation. When the sliding door in the back of the truck opened, three vamps ordered us to hop to the ground. A wave hit me like a splash of water in my face, and although the cold pricked my skin, it was also refreshing. I took a deep breath, filling my lungs. One hundred scents filled my nose with smells I've never considered before. It was my first breath of fresh air. Being kept inside filthy cages my whole life, the stench never bothered me because I never knew anything else. But now, a cool breeze tickled my neck, and the air cleared my sinuses as I inhaled again deeply through my nose.

A shove from behind broke my concentration, followed by a yell, "Let's go, let's go!" I obeyed the instructions and jumped to the ground. I found myself standing in a parking lot on the back side of a building.

I stumbled forward and noticed a vamp holding a door open with an impatient look on his face. Scanning the nondescript side of the building, there was no clue as to where they had taken us. Just a few dumpsters nearby. The man holding the door gave me a wide grin as I approached and said, "This one's cute, but looks can be deceiving. I hope the product is better than last time."

The vamp who brought us replied, "Oh, don't you worry, this batch is top-notch. We put new quality control protocols in place recently. Feel free to sample the merchandise."

We entered the building and found ourselves in a commercial kitchen. They led us to what looked like a walk-in refrigerator, except it was warm instead of cold. Our shivers turned to sweat from the heat that filled the small room. They attached our wrist cuffs to a wire running along the ceiling and left through a pair of double doors.

Before long, a vampire in a white outfit unlocked Jimmy from the wire and instructed him to lay on a metal table. He picked up a large knife, which he used to slice Jimmy's wrist, letting the arm dangle into a bucket on the floor. I watched the bucket fill with red liquid from Jimmy's veins. I lifted my gaze and met his eyes. Although he looked directly at me, his glazed over face focused on something in the distance. After a few seconds, his nervous twitches stopped. I was sure he was dead, but then he blinked again. Finally, a peaceful look came across his face. It might have been my imagination, but I swear his mouth cracked a smile as the last of his life dripped from his body.

I knew I should be outraged. I should scream and tear at my chains. But I just stood in silence, staring at Jimmy's dead body. Tears streamed down my cheeks, but I had no other physical reaction. Just like Jimmy in his last moments. Is it because we've been trained to submit? Or that we know our situation is hopeless? Maybe we just don't have enough energy left to put up a fight, as an individual or a species. I tried to scream, but no sound escaped my throat. I could hear the voices yelling inside my head. A thud snapped me out of my daydream as Jimmy's body fell to the ground and jerked across the floor. My eyes stayed glued to his lifeless body, wondering what was happening to him. Then I noticed the vamp dragging him out the door we had entered through. They had what they needed from him and it was time to dispose of the waste. The man in the white outfit returned for another one of my companions.

I prayed he would take me. I wanted to be chosen next and end this tortuous wait, but I would not be that lucky.

He laid the next girl on the table Jimmy occupied a minute earlier. I watched the same process repeat two more times until I was alone. My eyes stung from the tears that stained my cheeks. I realized in my final moments, I won't have a friendly face to look at, like my friends did. I'm truly all alone. The chef came to me and saw the look of defeat on my face. He said, "Don't worry. It will all be over soon. Besides, we have something different in store for you. Try to relax." He winked as he unlocked my shackles, but he laid me on the same table as the others.

I don't know why he bothered consoling me when my wrists were to be sliced in a matter of seconds. I don't need to be patronized. But instead of cutting me open like my friends, he fastened my arms and legs to the table. Then, using a large kitchen shears, he cut off my tattered clothes. I lay naked, strapped to a metal table, knowing this is how my story will end. The table moved. Its wheels rolled through the double doors into a small but elegant dining room with large red curtains draped on the walls. I turned my head to see tables and chairs made of plush black velvet, filled with eager vamps, dressed in lavish outfits I have only dreamed of. They grew silent as I came into view. I could feel their eyes burning into me as I lay before them.

The chef leaned over and whispered, "Try to be still. This will all be over soon. If you hadn't guessed, we serve dessert live."

The vampires seated around me held strange silver utensils I've never seen before. They resembled metal straws with sharp points at the end. Six of these straws plunged simultaneously into me. They dug deep into my flesh from all sides. Immense pain shot through my body. The vamps above me looked down, their mouths attached to the silver tubes, sucking the life from my body. Their moans of delight must mean they are enjoying me. I hope I taste as good as they expect. There is no point in resisting my fate. This is what I was born for.

V.E.T.H.

U nderground City
2115

Alec finished up his shift at work and headed to his car. He had a good day, even if it was extremely tiring. He enjoys his job, working at a non-profit, assisting the less fortunate. Something about helping people who can't speak up for themselves gives him a greater satisfaction than just offering himself for the highest salary.

Through his work, Alec assists in a variety of activities to support his company's causes. Lobbying politicians, who only offer help if they think it will look good for their next election, takes up much of his time. Public awareness campaigns are another large part of Alec's duties. He knows swaying public opinion is an uphill battle, but by constantly reminding everyone about the way these poor people live, maybe he can get through to some of them. Anything that brings media attention to their plight is fair game. Many consider Alec's organization to be comprised of far-left activists whose actions border domestic terrorism. Regardless of being in the slim minority, he knows his cause is just. The fulfillment Alec feels from his job is enough to keep him going, hoping he makes at least a slight difference, even though most of his efforts probably fall on deaf ears.

Although Alec likes his job, he also likes his time off. Exhausted from a long day at the office that included back-to-back meetings all afternoon, he is ready to enjoy the start of the weekend. Pressing a button on the dashboard, he dials his girlfriend Elise through the car's speaker while driving out of the parking lot.

"Hey babe, I'm just headed out now. What did you have in mind for tonight? I could stop by the store and pick something up or we could check out that new restaurant downtown. They've got excellent reviews and use all organic and local ingredients."

Elise's voice replied from the car speakers. Her voice was raised to compete with the background noise. "Alec! I'm out at Myst having a few drinks with Jenna for happy hour. Why don't you meet us down here and we'll go out to dinner after. Do you mind if she hangs with us tonight?"

"No problem, that sounds fine," Alec replied, knowing Elise already had their plans for the evening mapped out. "Let me stop home to freshen up, and I'll see you soon."

To say Elise is controlling is an understatement, but dating her had its advantages. Elise and Jenna were best friends and nearly inseparable. Although he wouldn't mind having more alone time with Elise, Jenna made him laugh and was more down to earth than his high-maintenance girlfriend. Alec pressed the end call button on his steering wheel and pushed his foot down on the accelerator. His car picked up speed and raced along the highway. A quick stop home, and he'd be chilling at the club with a drink in no time.

Alec lived in a third story flat in the older city. A minor inconvenience, but he had a good position on the waiting list for a prime spot in a new condominium being constructed. The building still needed some finishing touches before residents could move in, but it should be ready by the end of the year. He'd be able to breathe a little easier, living in a nicer neighborhood with better security, not to mention he would be closer to the nightlife scene where he had been hanging out recently, ever since he met Elise.

They've been dating about three months and met at one of the popular downtown clubs. Elise's father was old money, and she had become a well-known socialite with quite the reputation. She always had a lot of cash to spend, whether at the club or the high end department stores. Alec had been out after work with a few friends when Elise picked him out of the crowd. She sent an expensive bottle over to his table, a gesture she was known for. No one approached Elise or her friend without an invitation. If the girls were interested in talking to you, they would let you know. Elise was used to getting what she wanted and Alec certainly wasn't going to be the one to tell her no. He'd prefer some other poor soul be the one to catch her wrath. She looked good, after all. Her long, dark hair came down to her elbows and had a natural shine. Her enchanting green eyes sucked you in, making it extremely difficult to break away from her gaze. Alec was well aware of her reputation and figured the romance, if you could call it that, would likely be a one-night stand. Most of her boyfriends didn't last more than a week before they dropped off the radar, but to Alec's surprise, she let him stick around and before he knew it; they were a power couple. His face regularly appeared alongside hers on all the tabloids. Social media lit up with sightings of the duo whenever they were spotted out together. Although not Alec's normal scene, he came to enjoy the limelight.

Elise's father didn't feel the same way about Alec as his daughter. Being a high-profile aristocrat, he kept a close eye on his daughter and felt no qualms about sharing his opinions on the company she keeps. He immediately understood that Alec didn't come from a recognized and wealthy family, like he expected for his only daughter. Alec made a poor first impression, being unfamiliar with the etiquette of high society, and things only went downhill from there. Upon learning of Alec's work with the non-profit agency, Elise's father became incessant that she call off the relationship. A part of Alec thought Elise continued their romance just to get under her dad's skin and maybe there was some truth to that, but he might as well enjoy the ride while he had the chance. Who knows, maybe the old man will croak one of these days and Alec won't have to put up with his disapproving glares much longer.

Alec thought about his lucky streak while taking a quick shower before putting on an outfit appropriate for a night out. He selected a black silk button-up shirt with matching pants from his closet, a much more limited selection than his girlfriend's wardrobe. After getting dressed and putting on Elise's favorite cologne, he headed back out to meet the girls.

The club, located in a strip of similar nightlife and entertainment establishments, sat in one of the rowdiest sections of the city. The club's nouveau chic style and minimalist decor meant the owners kept the costs down and the prices high. In Alec's mind, the bar was the same as any other; except double the price and more pretentious pricks to deal with. Elise liked the vibe, though, and she paid the tab so he could deal with it.

He drove up to the entrance, where a valet hopped in his car and sped off to the parking lot around the corner. The bouncer knew Alec well and waved him in, allowing him to cut the line of revelers waiting their turn. A few of them grumbled as Alec walked by, but they knew better than to speak their mind to the bouncer if they wanted a chance of getting in at all.

Walking into the venue, he almost choked on the thick air. Fog machines worked overtime to pump the dense haze throughout the room. The music, although loud, didn't hurt the ears like some of the neighboring bars. A woman's hypnotizing voice sang from the speakers over a mellow electronic beat. Setting one foot into the fog felt like stepping into a magical new world. The humidity in the room gave the feeling of being outside in a forest, instead of inside a dingy building on a city block.

Even through the thick mist, Alec immediately spotted Elise waving at him from the center of the room. How could he miss her, in the middle of the dance floor, wearing a stunning sequin dress? Her friend Jenna danced alongside her, both of them showing off their moves and curves. Every guy, and most girls, in the room eyed the duo nervously. Most would kill for a chance to party with them for even one night, but knew the unwritten rule. They stayed just far enough away so as to not bother the girls while still trying to catch their eye. Anyone that attempted to dance with them without an invitation... well, good luck with that.

Alec took a step on the dance floor to meet them, but upon seeing him, they headed straight for the bar. "One more round of the special please, three this time," Elise said to the bartender as she approached.

Within a minute, the bartender had three metal shot glasses lined up and strained the concoction equally between them. The trio grabbed a glass and raised them together in a toast.

"To the weekend!" said Jenna.

Elise and Alec cheered simultaneously as they all drank the shots in a single gulp, slamming the metal glasses on the bar. The crowd parted before them as the three friends headed back to the dance floor. The music played on, soothing vocals and flashing lights mesmerized the crowd as the entire sea of people undulated in unison. After a few more songs and more than a few drinks, the group exited the club, looking for their next stop of the night.

"Did you guys want to get something to eat or....," Alec said, looking at Elise.

"Yeah sure, let's head over to Rare," she replied.

"Ok, but we always go there. I was hoping we might try that new place," Alec said.

"Well, I have a reservation already and the manager said next time I come in, he'll have something special for me," replied Elise. "Besides, I'm paying." With that, she swiveled and headed off down the street. Jenna followed close behind like a puppy dog, and Alec begrudgingly went as well.

Upon entering Rare, the manager, a close friend of Elise's father, greeted the group. He was a short, stocky man and looked like he spent a considerable amount of time at the gym each day. He gave Elise a big hug and a kiss on each cheek. In a thick accent, he said, "Elise, my darling, welcome. I've been waiting for you. I will have the chef bring you out his best meal. Please follow me to your table. We have a private room in the back waiting for you."

Within a minute of being seated, the server appeared, but instead of taking their orders, he asked if they were ready for him to bring the main course. Alec, confused since they hadn't even received menus yet, looked at his girlfriend. Sure, Elise might have preordered the special, but he preferred to choose his own meal. They had different palettes, and he didn't care for her controlling streak. Before he even had a chance to voice his concerns, Elise replied approvingly to the server, and he retreated to the kitchen to fetch their dinner, whatever that may be. Jenna seemed fine with being along for the ride and letting her friend call the shots, but Alec preferred to at least have some input.

The server returned a few minutes later. He held a metal chain in his hand that led to a leather collar. The collar was fastened around the neck of a young girl. She shuffled her feet along as the server led her into the room, keeping her head lowered. The manager poked his head in behind them. The girl couldn't have been more than sixteen years old, wearing only a ripped t-shirt with illegible writing. Wavy, strawberry blonde hair obscured most of her face. Wide with terror, one eye peeked from between tufts of hair. Jenna jumped with glee as she saw the girl being led in. "O-M-G, a live human! How did you manage that?" she asked her friend.

Elise laughed at the question. "I thought I'd surprise you guys. Daddy promised me this as a late birthday present and there's no one I'd rather enjoy it with than you two."

The manager smiled at the girls' delight. He liked a satisfied customer, especially one with parents as rich as hers. He bid the girls farewell and left them to enjoy their meal in peace.

The young girl, hearing Elise and Jenna's conversation, realized at once their intent. "Please... don't kill me. I... You can keep me... I'll be your servant."

This elicited chuckles from Elise and Jenna. "Nice idea. I would love a pet," said Elise, "but it's too risky. Everyone knows it's illegal to keep humans at home. We'd rather just enjoy you right now. Isn't that right guys? I was never one to save leftovers."

Jenna didn't need a second invitation as she approached the girl, running her tongue along the edge of her exposed fang. Her bright red lips glistened with saliva at the thought of tasting the forbidden fruit. A living human.

After the vampire uprising, an exponential increase in the undead population forced the new authority to issue laws regarding human consumption. With a dwindling worldwide human population, killing for a meal was strictly forbidden. Many of the older vampires who believed in traditional values had a hard time coming to terms with the new rules and way of life, but eventually, most of them came around. They understood the benefits of living outside the shadows. Being in charge outweighed the drawbacks of controlled feedings. If used correctly, vampire food is a renewable resource, but the indiscriminate killing needed to end to ensure the blood supply remained plentiful. These regulations required the vampires to breed and process the limited human population at farms to maximize the blood output of each person. Factory farms popped up all over the globe and vampire scientists engineered a specialized feed to improve blood recovery rates. All of this ensured a constant supply of fresh blood would always be available. The main bottleneck in this process was that baby humans take so long to mature. It takes over a decade before a human child is large enough for sufficient blood to be harvested. To mitigate this, hormones were developed to increase the growth rate of young humans. These hormones, if introduced from birth, allowed humans to reach maturity by six years old. Tests were still underway to determine if the hormones affected the human's lifespan.

Ensuring the vampire population of the world remains fed is a large job with many cogs in the process. Any disruption to the food chain could prove deadly to their species. Luckily for the vampires, RedLife already had collection and distribution channels working smoothly through their voluntary donation program. A few minor changes to the process allowed them to integrate breeding and raising humans to their operations. By no longer needing to find new ways to entice humans to hand over their blood willingly, their operation became more efficient, which it needed to be if they had any hope of feeding all the new vampires.

Until recently, many farms rented out their livestock to expensive restaurants and high-class dinner parties. At these exclusive events, the vampires could feed from, but not kill, a human, under strict supervision. For the wealthy, drinking directly from the vein was worth every penny. The security present at these events ensured the humans survived to serve the next client.

A new strain of vampire herpes put an end to these dinner parties. This new disease spread quickly at these events, raising fears of a vampire pandemic. The tainted blood sickened infected vampires, who became ill after consuming it. Many even died the true death, causing a mass panic. Fear of this disease spread rapidly throughout society and new legislation quickly passed the Vampire Parliament banning all live human consumption. Anyone caught taking part in these so called 'feeding parties' would be executed at first light. Companies who made a killing off these events became furious and fought to keep them legal with stricter safety protocols in place. Regardless of the pushback, the parliament, fearing for the species' survival, put an end to the practice.

The scene in front of Alec played out in a matter of seconds. Emotions swirled in his head, overflowing like a boiling pot. They bubbled over with shock, anger, and confusion. Elise was well aware of his feelings about human cruelty and his non-profit work with V.E.T.H. This was a slap in the face to everything that *Vampires for the Ethical Treatment of Humans* stood for. The organization advocated for better living conditions in human farms as well as preventing needless torture and abuse of the people kept there. V.E.T.H. prided itself on being one of the driving forces that outlawed live human consumption in the first place.

Alec glanced over at Elise and caught her watching him. She made no attempt to hide her stare and smiled at his contemptuous look, waiting for his next move. She was testing him, and he had a decision to make. He looked at the young girl who stood before them. Her lips trembled and her whole body visibly shook with fright. Being a new vampire, compared to many in the community, and living in the modern age of vampire rule, Alec had never fed from a live human before. He had no qualms admitting that he was far removed from the predatory roots of his species. Truth be told, Alec was glad not to have to hunt himself, preferring instead to pick up a case of blood packs at the grocery store. There was something to be said for the conveniences of modern day life. Some vampires might consider him weak and unworthy of the undead gift. But Alec was a lover, not a killer, and he felt sorrow for the quivering girl in front of them.

Elise took notice of the battle going on in his head and attempted to help sway his mind. "Go for it Alec, this is a once in a lifetime opportunity. It's what our species is meant to do. She's all natural. For all your talk about locally sourced blood, you can't get more farm to table than this. Look at her. Listen. Can't you hear the blood pumping through her pathetic veins? It's asking to be let out. You know you want just a tiny taste. I bet she's delicious."

Instead of tuning in on the sound of the girl's blood flow, he focused on her quick and labored breaths. A single sharp inhale through her nose followed by multiple small exhales from her mouth showed the anxiety that tormented her. Alec knew a refusal here would mean the end of his relationship with Elise, but he realized now that they were incompatible. He talked with Elise often about his work, and she never indicated a problem with his activism. He was shocked she would do something like this. She must have known what his reaction would be. The urge to get up and walk out of the room came over him, but he couldn't allow them to tear this little girl to shreds.

Knowing nothing less than a physical confrontation would keep these two from the girl, Alec tried another angle. "Let's have our fun with her, but let her live so we can enjoy her again. Humans are scarce these days and it seems like a waste to kill one for a snack."

Elise shook her head with disappointment and disgust. "I expected better from you. Don't be such a wimp," she said. "We're meant to feast on these pitiful humans. They're nothing but bags of blood to us."

"Just because we need something to survive doesn't make it right. Especially when we can get what we need in a more humane way," Alec replied.

"Humane!" she repeated with a loud laugh. "What an archaic word."

At that point, Alec came to his senses, realizing he had no chance of saving the human. Even if he fended off the two salivating vampires in the room and made it past the restaurant's security, where would he bring the girl so that she would be safe? If he just let them do what they wanted with her, he could break it off with Elise later and consider his options from there. It was not worth making a scene at the restaurant and jeopardizing his own safety.

Looking back at the girl, he saw the fear and sadness in her eyes, a dejected look as if she had given up all hope. It pained him to see this poor creature in front of him, aware of the vampires' intentions and listening in as they debated her fate.

Alec took in a deep breath, looked at Elise and said, "Go ahead. I'm not in the mood. I'm feeling a little weird from those shots at the bar, but enjoy." His words rang hollow because his thoughts lay elsewhere. Wondering about questions that he had no answers for. *At what point does a level of consciousness and comprehension make the act of killing these humans barbaric? Are vampires inherently evil, as the humans suggest? Or are we just a new species at the top of the food chain, the result of evolution? Maybe Elise is right. There is no point in fighting against our nature.*

By now, Jenna had the girl backed into a corner and gripped her by the shoulder. Her sharpened claws dug deep into the girl's skin, causing blood to dribble down her arm from each puncture. Jenna's attention lay on the arguing couple as her nails burrowed deeper into the girl's flesh. The girl sank to her knees while blood continued to spill from the wounds on her shoulder. Jenna impatiently waited for her friend to give the final approval to chow down.

Finally, Elise said, "Alec should do the honors. I Insist." Her eyes, still locked on his, waiting for a reaction. She seemed to enjoy taunting him this way.

Jenna, irritated by the on-again, off-again drama, just wanted to get on with the meal. She didn't care who took the first bite. She heaved the girl in Alec's direction, causing her to stumble before falling to her knees again.

The girl looked up at him, tears rolling down her cheeks, and whimpered, "Please, just get it over with."

Alec's eyes watered as well, but he held back his tears, reminding himself this sort of thing probably still happens all the time. He was foolish for thinking he could make a difference when even his own girlfriend was so callous. He stood up, walking past the girl towards the exit and said, "Whatever. Do what you want, but I don't have to listen to you or obey your commands. We're done."

Elise shook her head and said, "I knew Daddy was right all along."

Just as Alec grabbed hold of the door, it burst open, knocking away into his outstretched hand. Alec gasped in surprise as Elise's father, along with two large bodyguards entered the room.

The bodyguards went right for Alec, each taking hold of one arm. Alec looked at Elise's father in shock at the sudden intrusion. They entered at just the right time. Alec's eyes darted to the ceiling at the small black housing of a security camera. They had been watching the entire time. He wondered how many people were in on this illegal operation.

Alec couldn't move, held in place by the thugs, his arms being pulled in opposite directions. He strained his neck to the side and saw Elise walking around the room. She accepted an object from her father and turned to face Alec.

"What are you going to do? Let me go, you know I won't say anything, babe," Alec said to Elise, trying to diffuse the situation. He glimpsed the object she held as she stepped closer to him. To his surprise, nestled in her palm was an ornate wooden stake. The hand carved piece looked to be hundreds of years old. The carvings resembled a bramble of roots, twisting around the stake. Even though the ancient relic looked like it belonged in a museum, the sharp point at the tip remained deadly.

Their eyes met and Alec conveyed a look of shock that she would even joke about something like this. The past few months together had meant something to him. Even if they weren't compatible, they didn't have to end it this way. Apparently, none of that mattered to her. She was ready to end the relationship with a bang. He refused to believe she would go through with it, convincing himself that this was another one of her tests. Maybe she would spare him at the last second and spite her father, but as she neared, he saw the deadly look in her eyes. She proceeded with the look of someone who had done this many times before. He knew then he had made a fatal mistake.

"Well, I guess it's back to the dating pool. There's always more fish in the sea," said Elise as she leaned into Alec and slid the stake through the nicest shirt in his wardrobe.

Their lips connected as the stake pressed through his flesh, tearing through his pectoral muscle and piercing his heart. She pushed her tongue into his mouth as he gasped for air. The stake tore through the back side of his vital organ, prodding the tissue behind it. She gave him one last kiss as she felt his lips begin to wither. She withdrew before getting too much of the foul taste on her tongue, but kept her eyes locked with his as his final moment passed.

"Now, where were we?" she said, and turned to the girl still cowering in the corner. "That excitement really worked up my appetite."

Ode To Death

Listen up, and gather round
While you're here, don't make a sound
I have a lesson, that I must share
Disregard, if you dare
But I have lived, long enough
There is no need, for me to bluff
The length of time, I've been alive
No one else, has survived
I've been around, the entire planet
Explored every cave, made of granite
After all these years, as of yet
Every man, I've ever met
Has the same, aspiration
To live for every, Earth rotation
They would like, to live forever
Proud at such, a good endeavor
This is their true, deepest desire
But since they can't, they must sire
As many children, as they can

To spread their seed, expand their clan
But if I said, there was a way
To live forever, without seeing day
Would you agree, to this stipulation
Obtaining blood, your main fixation
Always hungry, like a shark
And only prowling, in the dark
Watching your friends, wither away
After they are gone, you must stay
It's fine at first, on the hunt
But your social skills, will surely stunt
And live too long, on your own
With no one left, to share your throne
You will forget, what makes you a man
And say goodbye, to your tan
Maybe you, will have better luck
At enjoying life, without being stuck
So for me, I'm near the end
I've seen it all, lived every trend
And while I wait, around to die
Ask me now, I will not lie
What is it, you want to know
I'll tell all, before I go
Of course it's true, that at first
Your new life, is not the worst
As long as you, do not mind
Drinking blood, of your own kind
And for the first, one hundred years
You'll leave behind, shed your fears
Hunting in, the dead of night
Your prey will not, put up a fight
But if you are, a little queasy

This new life, might not come easy
Once you start, to feel the thirst
You'll understand, that it's a curse
And this is why, I refused to share
This awful fate, with my only heir
Whom of course, has passed away
Two hundred years, ago this day
Maybe you, will understand
When you see, my wedding bands
Each one of these, my lovely wives
I live on, when none survived
Oh to lay, with them in peace
I truly wish, to be deceased
I no longer want, to walk this Earth
I've lived my life, for all it's worth
As you hear, my final song
I pray you under, stand its wrong
To stay alive, forevermore
It's not just that, life is a bore
It also has, become a chore
To live a life, that's full of gore

Acknowledgments

Thanks to my amazing wife Amellia, for allowing me to pursue this dream and putting up with my bizarre antics. My daughter for cheering me on and my son for jumping on me anytime I try to write. :)

My beta readers: Alexa K Moon, Mechelle Lee, Heather Ann Larson, Amanda Worthington, Catherine & Jeremy Blain, Sagnik Sinha, Ollie Gill, and Lizzy Roth. Thanks for all your feedback in helping me shape this book and encouraging me to continue.

Special thanks to anyone who has posted, commented or liked a post in the Books of Horror group on Facebook over the past two years. Without the readers and authors in BoH, this book wouldn't exist.

and thank you to anyone reading this for giving a new author a chance.

About Author

LM Kaplin is a new author from upstate New York who has been a horror enthusiast in all forms his entire life. His morbid obsession with the macabre started one night while watching Poltergeist as a young child. The next morning, he began searching for ancient burial grounds in the backyard. Dismayed at not uncovering any evil spirits, he buried his own demons for future generations to find. It's time to start digging them up.

Find him on Facebook or Instagram or email him at LMKaplin@gmail.com

If you enjoyed this book, please consider leaving a review on Amazon, GoodReads, or your favorite social media platform.